Road to
Christmas Past

By

Kathi Daley

D1733482

This book is a work of fiction. Names, characters, places and incidents either are products of the author's imagination or are used fictitiously. Any resemblance to actual events or locales or persons, living or dead, is entirely coincidental.

Copyright © 2013 by Katherine Daley

Version 1.0

This book is dedicated to my mom, who taught me the importance of family.

I also want to thank Christy for her valuable feedback, Ricky for the webpage, Randy Ladenheim-Gil for the editing, Paul for the encouragement, and, last but not least, my super-husband Ken for allowing me time to write by taking care of everything else.

Other Books by Kathi Daley

Available on Amazon

Paradise Lake Series:
Pumpkins in Paradise
Snowmen in Paradise – coming
January 2014

Zoe Donovan Mysteries:
Halloween Hijinks
The Trouble With Turkeys
Christmas Crazy
Cupid's Curse – **coming January 2014**

Chapter 1

Tuesday, November 26

"Four shots, nonfat, extra hot, no foam." Holly Thompson's tall, dark-haired assistant, Jessica Stewart, set a latte in front of her. "Whole wheat bagel with cream cheese on the side and today's letters." She set those next to the cup. "My favorite is on the top."

Holly, a petite blonde with blue eyes and a sunny smile, tucked a lock of her long hair behind her ear, adjusted the glasses on her nose, and picked up the letter from the top of the stack. She glanced at the letter while Jessica perched on the side of her desk, sipping from her own coffee.

For the past three years, Holly had worked as an advice columnist for a popular weekly women's magazine. Her commitment to offering practical solutions to complex situations set her apart from other advice columns, sending her reader share to the top of the charts.

"Looks good," Holly commented after scanning the handwritten note. "Get me the woman's contact information and we'll see where it goes. Do I have any messages?"

"Actually, yes." Jessica set down her legal pad and pulled a note out of her pocket. "Phillip wanted me to remind you that he needs your copy early this week due to the holiday weekend."

"Holiday weekend?"

"Thanksgiving," Jessica reminded her.

"Oh, yeah. Go on."

"Kira wants to know if you got the tickets for the benefit next month, and Derek left a message asking if you wanted to do lunch."

"Tell Phillip he'll have next week's column by the end of the day. Call Derek and tell him I'll have to take a rain check on lunch, then call and get four tickets to the PETA benefit next month. If you're able to get the tickets, call Kira, see where she wants to have dinner, and make the reservations. Things tend to get busy in December. Oh, and see if you can find me a date."

"A date? What kind of date?"

Holly shrugged. "The benefit is black tie, so preferably someone who has a black tie. Other than that, use your discretion."

"You don't want to go with Derek?"

"Derek?" Holly frowned.

"Derek Quinn," Jessica reminded her. "The man you've been dating for the past five months."

"Derek and I aren't dating. We're just . . ."

"Colleagues," Jessica said, anticipating her response.

"Friends," Holly countered.

Jessica smiled patiently, as she would at a child who was a little slow. "I'm sorry to break this to you, but you're dating. Ask anyone."

Holly frowned as she tried to digest what Jessica was telling her.

"For someone who gives absolutely brilliant answers to others concerning their love lives, you are totally clueless when it comes to your own," Jessica teased. "For future reference, when a very eligible single man takes you to dinner several times a week, showers you with gifts for absolutely no reason, and sends flowers on a regular basis, you're dating."

"Derek gave me one necklace he brought back from his trip to Paris. He doesn't shower me with gifts."

"Maybe not, but trust me, as far as he's concerned, you're dating. In fact, the entire third floor is involved in a pool to predict when he'll pop the question."

"Don't be ridiculous," Holly snorted. "We haven't even . . ." Holly paused, and Jessica simply smiled at her boss's discomfort. "Well, you know. Still, I guess I should talk to him."

"I think that might be a good idea."

Holly sighed. She hated to ruin the friendship she thought she had with Derek by pointing out to him that she was in no way interested in any type of serious relationship, but she supposed she owed him some clarification. It wasn't that Derek wasn't perfectly datable. He was indeed quite the catch, but Holly didn't have time to date. She had goals, ambitions, and a timeline that didn't account for a serious relationship for at least another five years.

"Anything else?" Holly asked.

"Noel's on line three and Warren just called up from the lobby. I gather we have a very interesting delivery on the way up."

"Interesting how?"

Jessica shrugged. "I don't know. He didn't say, but he was snickering, so I'm guessing it isn't your normal brown box."

"Okay." Holly picked up her latte. "I'll talk to Noel while I drink my coffee. Buzz me when the delivery gets here."

"Hey, Noel," Holly greeted Noel Davis, her best friend in the entire world. Leaning back in her chair, she swiveled around so that her back was to her door and she was able to look out of the window. "Hope Jessica didn't keep you waiting too long."

"It's okay. I was making the kids' lunches while I waited," Noel said. "I know it's early, but I wanted to catch you before you got too busy. I really need to finalize our plans for next month."

"Next month?"

"Christmas, silly. We're going to have the best time this year. There is so much I need to tell you."

Holly knew that the Davis household was probably already decked out in Christmas attire, even though there was still two days until Thanksgiving.

"Remember, I told you that Donny married that socialite from Manhattan?" Noel continued without waiting for Holly's reply. "Well, you'll never guess what happened..."

Holly stared at the skyline outside the window of her New York City office as Noel droned on about the latest news from her hometown of Moosehead, Minnesota. Normally, Holly loved catching up with her former foster sister, but since Meg's death, tales of Donny Preston's new wife and the plans for the Winter Ball had failed to hold her interest the way they once had.

Holly tried to listen, but talking to Noel brought back memories she hadn't found the courage to deal with quite yet. She picked up the picture of Aunt Meg that she kept on her desk and ran a finger over it. Aunt Meg was the only mother she had ever known. Holly had come to live in her large home filled with foster kids when she was only a few days old and had stayed until she left for college.

"Sounds great," she answered distractedly as she watched an early snow start to fall, "but I just don't know if I can get away. Things are sort of hectic this year." Holly rustled some of the folders on her desk for effect. "I have a million letters to read, and there's a rumor going around that we might enter into talks to syndicate my column."

"That's great, Holly. I'm so happy for you. I really am, but still . . ." Noel jumped right in to what sounded like a rehearsed speech concerning the importance of balance in one's life.

Tears filled Holly's eyes as she remembered the previous Thanksgiving. She'd come home, as she had every year, to a house filled with love and laughter and the smell of pumpkin pie baking in the oven. She'd settled into her old room, then headed into town with Meg to help prepare the feast that would be served to those less fortunate in the town's community center. After everyone had been served, she'd sat down with Meg, and they'd shared a meal, just the two of them.

Friday had been tree-cutting day with Noel and her family, and Saturday she'd helped Meg decorate the huge farmhouse that, until a couple of years earlier, had housed a handful of foster kids at any given time. She loved Moosehead and missed the traditions there, but without Meg nothing would be the same.

"Holly, are you still there?" Noel interrupted her daydreams.

"I'm here."

"So about Clay . . . What should I tell him?"

Clay? Holly racked her brain, trying to remember what Noel had been rambling on about. Oh, yes, the blind date.

"As appealing as this guy sounds, I'm going to have to see how things go. I really can't make any promises at this point."

"But you always come home for Christmas," Noel said.

"Yeah, I know. But things are . . ." Holly looked down at the eight-by-ten photo she still held, "different this year."

Noel paused. "I know. But if you don't want to stay out at Meg's, you can stay with us. We'd love to have you."

"You have a rather large husband, four children under the age of ten, two dogs, four cats, and six goldfish, and you live in a shoebox," Holly reminded her. "As much as I love you and your family, there's no way you have room for a houseguest over the Christmas holiday."

"There's always the couch," Noel suggested.

"If I come to Moosehead for Christmas, and that's a big *if*," Holly cautioned, "I'll stay at Aunt Meg's. I guess I'm going to have to come home and figure out what to do with the place at some point anyway. It was really sweet of her to leave me the house, but honestly, I'm not sure I want it."

"Holly," Noel whispered, "Aunt Meg loved you. She loved all her kids, but she loved you the most. She wanted you to have the house. It's your home."

"*Was* my home," Holly reminded her. "I live in New York now."

"You could move back. To Moosehead, I mean. You have the house, and I'm sure the local newspaper would hire you. And if that doesn't work out, I'm sure we can find you something else."

"It's not that I'm worried about finding a job," Holly clarified. "It's just that Moosehead isn't my home anymore. New York is."

"Home is where your family is." Noel sounded sad.

"You know I love you," Holly assured Noel. "You mean more to me than any other person on this planet, and we'll always be family, but sometimes—uh, hang on." Holly paused, holding her hand over the mouthpiece of the phone as Jessica poked her head in through her office door.

"Your delivery is here," Jessica informed her. "It's an early Christmas present."

"Just put it on the table with the others," Holly instructed.

"It's uh . . ." Jessica paused, "rather large. I think you should come take a look. This is definitely something you're going to want to see."

"Okay, I'll be right there. Sorry," Holly said, returning her attention to Noel. "I have some kind of delivery that requires my attention. I should go."

"Okay." Noel sounded reluctant to let her friend hang up before she could wrangle a commitment out of her to come home for the holidays. "Thanksgiving is the day after tomorrow. I can just picture you curling up in your tiny apartment with a frozen turkey dinner and a martini with extra olives. You'll put on some old movie and fall asleep on your couch snuggled up with that life-size bed pillow you bought last time we went shopping. If you can get a flight into Minneapolis, I'll come pick you up."

"Thanks for the offer, but I really need to stay here and get some work done. Besides, I have plans," Holly lied. "A friend invited me to Thanksgiving dinner, so I won't be alone."

"Are we talking a friend of the male gender?" Noel asked.

"Yes, so you see, I'm fine."

"Tell me everything."

"I love you, but I really have to go."

"I love you, too. I miss you. Please come home," Noel pleaded.

"I'll try. I'll call you next week and we'll talk about it."

"Okay. Have fun at Thanksgiving. Call me when you get home from your date. I want all the details."

"I'll try, but it might be late."

"Then call me the next morning. Assuming you'll be at home the next morning," Noel drawled seductively.

"I'll be home." Holly grinned as she slammed down the phone.

Holly set the picture of Aunt Meg back down on her desk and buzzed Jessica. "So about this delivery . . . ?"

"Stay there; I'll bring it in."

Holly took a sip of her latte as Jessica opened the door connecting her office to the reception area and ushered in the most gorgeous man Holly had ever seen. She almost choked on her coffee as she stared speechlessly at the tall, dark-haired man, who had eyes bluer than her own, was dressed all in black, and had a huge red bow taped to his chest.

"Can I help you?" she croaked as she stood up from behind her desk, straightening the short skirt of the gray business suit that had cost her a month's salary.

"Ms. Thompson, my name is Ben Holiday." His eyes crinkled as he beamed a lopsided smile and introduced himself. "I'm your Christmas present from Meg."

"Meg?" Holly nervously tucked her long blonde hair behind one ear as she tried to wrap her mind around what the beautiful man was talking about. "Meg's dead," she informed him.

"I know. She made the arrangements before she . . . passed."

"Meg bought you for me?"

"Actually, she won me. In a poker game."

"She won you?"

"Yes, ma'am."

Holly stared at the strange man in front of her, then started to laugh. "You've got to be kidding."

"Afraid not."

"Did Noel send you?" Holly laughed harder.

"No. Like I said, Meg made all the arrangements."

"She won you in a poker game?" She grinned.

"Yes, ma'am."

Holly studied the man in front of her. Broad shoulders, an apparently flat stomach behind the red bow, long legs, and the warmest smile she had ever seen. *Thank you, Aunt Meg.*

"So now what? You said you were my Christmas present. Are you going to wash my dishes and vacuum my rugs?"

"Not exactly. More like you have use of my professional services between now and Christmas, free of charge, thanks to Meg and a straight flush."

"Services?" Holly choked.

"Perhaps you should open the box." The beautiful man handed her a small box wrapped in bright green paper. "It's the second half of the present. Although . . ." He hesitated. "Maybe this isn't the best time."

"Now's as good a time as any." Holly shrugged as she took the box and ripped open the shiny wrapping paper. Inside were a DVD and two matching necklaces that looked old and expensive. They each prominently featured a large sapphire surrounded by diamonds that were placed artistically on a latticework of intricate gold design. Holly picked up one of the necklaces, then looked at the man, who had sat down on the chair opposite her desk.

"Do you have a DVD player in here?"

"Yes. It's in the cabinet in the corner."

Ben got up from the chair, walked across the room, and opened the cabinet to reveal a DVD player, as well as a small television. He slipped the tape into the player and hesitated.

"Are you sure you want to do this now? The whole thing might be rather emotional."

"Yeah, I'm sure."

Ben pushed play, and a screen-size image of Meg sitting in the rocker on her front porch appeared. "Holly," she began speaking, "my beautiful child. Before I begin what is to be a fairly long and probably life-altering story, I want you to know that I love you with all my heart. Many children have passed through my life over the years, and I've loved each and every one of them, but you are the only one who is truly mine."

A single tear slid down Holly's cheek. Ben pulled his chair around so that he was sitting beside her and put his arm around her shoulders, pulling her as close as the bulky chairs would allow.

"We can do this later."

"Let it play."

"What I am about to tell you is probably something I should have told you long ago," Meg continued. "I meant to. First I was waiting for you to get old enough to understand the significance of what I'm about to tell you, and then I was waiting for the right moment, a moment that somehow never came."

Meg paused and looked away from the camera, as if trying to work up the courage to continue. Holly waited as Meg took several deep breaths before looking into the camera once more.

"Please don't hate me for keeping this from you for all these years," she gasped, "and please don't hate me for telling you now. Remember that no matter what your feelings are about what I'm going to tell you, I love you with all my heart and have always tried to do what I thought was best for you."

Ben wiped a tear from Holly's cheek with the side of his finger as one tear turned into many. Seeing Meg, hearing her speak for the first time since she'd died, was almost more than Holly's fragile heart could take. God, how she missed her.

"When you were five years old and Noel came to live with us, you asked me for the first time about your own parents," Meg continued. "I told you that you came to me when you were only a few days old, and that your parents had been killed in a terrible auto accident, which left them so badly burned that their identities were never discovered. The police searched for months, but every lead turned out to be a dead end. Since you had no name, I named you Holly, and I gave you my own last name, Thompson."

Meg hesitated, as if trying to pull her thoughts together. "I know you've always wondered about your birth parents: who they were, where you come from. When I beat Ben in a poker game and won his services for a month, I saw my opportunity not only to set things straight but to try to help you find your answers." Meg smiled as she glanced at something or someone beyond the camera. Probably Ben, if, as Holly supposed, he was the one taping Meg's final message to her.

"Ben is a lousy poker player, one of the worst I've ever come across, but he's an excellent private detective. If you decide you want to proceed with your search for your birth parents, you will have the use of his services for the next month. Before you decide whether or not to proceed with that project, there are a few things you need to know."

"I can't believe you bet yourself in a poker game." Holly chuckled through her tears. "If you were totally out of money, why didn't you just fold?"

"I wasn't out of money."

"Then why did you bet yourself instead of using tens and twenties, like a normal person?"

"That's a story for another day."

Meg started crying, bringing Holly's focus back to the screen. "She looks so sad."

"Scared."

"Why?"

"You'll see. Just keep watching."

"When you asked me about your parents . . ." Her voice cracked. "What I told you was true but not, I'm afraid, the entire story. The accident that brought you into my life happened on a dark country road during a blizzard that lasted for days. God must have been with you that night, because the likelihood of another vehicle traveling on the same dark, snowy road was remote. But, as luck would have it, a motorist did happen across the vehicle in which you were traveling just moments after the accident occurred. No one really knows what caused the car to go out of control and roll before coming to rest in a snowbank, but the accident was a bad one, and the other occupants of the vehicle were dead before the motorist happened by."

Holly stared intently at the screen as Meg continued. "The car was leaking gas, and just as the motorist pulled you out of the backseat, it burst into flames. The infant seat you were traveling in had protected you from most of the impact from the accident, and although your little body suffered cuts and bruises, you basically came out of the ordeal without serious injury. The others, however, perished in the fire."

Meg hesitated before continuing. "Everything that I've told you to this point you already know, since I've shared all of this with you at some point in the past. There are, however, a few things I haven't told you about the accident."

Meg stopped rocking and sat forward. Holly could see that she was gripping the armrests of the chair so tightly that her knuckles were turning white. She opened her mouth several times, as if to speak, then stopped and hesitated, as if unsure whether she should continue.

"The motorist who pulled you out told the police that there were two infant seats in the backseat of the car, and two diaper bags. He told the police that both diaper bags held infant-size diapers and clothes, as well as bottles and formula, but that the second infant seat was empty."

"Oh, God." Holly went pale as Meg struggled to continue with her story. Ben laced his fingers through Holly's in a gesture of support.

"The motorist managed to get you and both diaper bags out of the car before it burst into flames. He searched the area as best as he was able on a dark night in the middle of a blizzard before speeding to the next town, where he dropped you at a hospital and notified the police of the accident and the missing baby."

Meg wiped the steady flow of tears from her face as she spoke. "The police conducted an extensive search, but another baby was never found. It isn't known whether a second baby was even in the car at the time of the accident. Lack of any remains indicated that the second infant seat was empty at the time of the accident, but that doesn't explain the second diaper bag.

"I know you're probably in shock right now, but I'm afraid there's more. After the bodies, or should I say what was left of the bodies of your parents, were recovered, they were sent to a forensic scientist in the hopes of identifying them. While actual identities were never determined, it was discovered that, although you couldn't have been more than forty-eight hours old at the time of the accident, the woman in the car showed no signs of having given birth," Meg paused, "ever."

Holly stared at the screen, unable to speak. She held on to Ben's hand as if it was her only lifeline to sanity as Meg continued.

"They don't know the identity of the couple who died in the fire, but they're certain they weren't your biological parents. The authorities tried for months to discover your identity, looking through birth records and trying to match your footprint with those on record at nearby hospitals. It was finally concluded that you must have been born outside the hospital system, since no paper trail seemed to exist. There have been many theories as to what occurred that night, but no one knows for sure. Ben has agreed to help you look into the matter if you choose to do so. The chances of finding out any more than the police did twenty-seven years ago are slim, but Ben is one of the smartest and most capable people I've ever known, and if anyone can find out the truth, it's him. The only clues I have to offer are the two necklaces that were included with this tape. They were packed away in the two identical diaper bags that were found that night."

Meg dried her eyes and sat back in her chair. "I guess that's all. I know I've dumped a lot on you. I wish I were there to help you through this. If you decide not to pursue the search for what happened that night, I completely understand. Either way, Ben is yours for the month, so enjoy him. I love you, Hollybell."

The screen went blank.

"Holly? Are you okay? Can I get you anything? Do anything for you?"

Holly continued to stare at the blank screen. She didn't move, couldn't breathe.

"I know it's a lot to take in. Meg was really nervous about telling you the whole story. I don't think she could do it before. I think the secret has haunted her for years."

Holly looked up and stared directly into Ben's deep blue eyes. "I might have a sister. Or maybe a brother. And possibly parents," Holly whispered, so quietly that Ben could barely hear her. "How could she have kept that from me?"

Ben tucked a stray lock of hair behind Holly's ear before answering. "I don't think she meant to. I think the years just got away from her. Meg loved you. She didn't want you to be hurt. Even if we decide to look for them, the chances of finding out the truth are slim. We have very little to go on."

"I guess we'd better get started then." *Emotionally fragile Holly* was quickly replaced by *Get-the-job-done Holly.* "I'll need to talk to my boss to arrange for a leave of absence. We're getting ready to shut down in a couple of weeks for the holiday break, so I should be able to negotiate something until after the first of the year. Here's my address," she said, handing him a piece of paper on which she had scribbled the address of her apartment. "Meet me there in a few hours and we'll figure out what our first move is."

After handing Ben the paper, Holly picked up her phone, effectively dismissing him in the process. "Jessica," she spoke into the receiver, "I need you to do a few things for me, but first buzz Phillip and tell him I need to see him right away. Oh, and bring my calendar with you when you come in. We'll need to cancel all my appointments for the remainder of the year."

"So where do we start?" she asked Ben two hours later, as she poured two martinis.

"Actually, I took the liberty of checking out a few things before our meeting today. I figured if you wanted to pursue the search, we'd be that much ahead, and if you didn't, no harm done."

"I definitely want to pursue the search," Holly assured him. "What'd you find out?" She stabbed one of the several olives in her frosty glass with a blue toothpick, plucked out the pimento, tossed it in the ashtray beside her, and nibbled on the large, vodka-soaked fruit.

"You don't like pimentos?"

"Hate 'em."

"Seems like a lot of work to dig them out."

"I don't mind. Now about the case . . . ?"

"My investigation turned up several interesting things, including the identity of the man who found you in the wrecked car. He name is John Remington and he's still alive and living in Fargo, North Dakota. I tried to phone him, but it seems he's been living in a nursing home since he suffered a partial memory loss due to a brain tumor a few years ago. The attendant I spoke with says he has good days and bad, and the best chance we have of getting any information out of him is to visit him personally and hope for a good day."

"I'll call the airlines."

"I don't fly."

"What?"

"I was in an airplane accident when I was ten," Ben explained. "My father died and I was trapped inside the plane with his body for two days before they found me. I haven't flown since."

"Oh, God, I'm sorry. That must have been horrible. Was he your only family?"

"No, my mother and four sisters were safe at home. My mom remarried two years later, and I had a relatively normal childhood, considering. The only permanent scar I seem to have from the whole experience is my total aversion to flying. We'll have to drive."

"But it's almost fifteen hundred miles. It'll take days."

"Have you ever driven across country before?"

"No, I can't say that I have."

"It's beautiful. You'll enjoy it. Now, pack a bag and we'll head out first thing tomorrow morning. The earlier the better. How about I pick you up around five?"

"A.M.?"

"A.M. I'll bring coffee. Here's my cell number, in case you need to contact me between now and then. Since we don't really know where this journey will take us, bring clothes for both warm and cold climates and sturdy shoes. Oh, and bring the necklaces. They may provide us with valuable clues if we can just figure out what we're looking for." Ben kissed her on the cheek and headed toward the door.

"Wait. You're leaving? I thought you said you found out several things. What else besides the identity of the man who rescued me as an infant?"

"Like you said, we have days of traveling ahead of us. We'll talk on the way. Now, have a good dinner, pack sensibly, and get to bed early. Five o'clock comes mighty early on a cold fall morning."

"I like lattes. Nonfat."

Ben looked at her as if completely baffled by what she was trying to communicate to him. "You said you'd bring coffee. I prefer lattes. Venti, with four shots and no foam. Starbucks has red cups this time of year. Very festive. There's one down the street. I think they're open twenty-four hours."

"Check. One Venti, four shots, nonfat latte with no foam in a red cup from Starbucks. Anything else?"

"No, that'll do it."

"Okay, I'll see you in the morning. Try to get some rest. I think we're going to be in for a long month."

After Ben left, Holly sat down on the new leather sofa she couldn't afford. "Oh my God," she whispered as everything started to sink in. Her entire life, she had operated under the assumption that her parents were dead and she was alone in the world. Not that she was ever really alone. She'd always had Meg. She knew that Meg loved her as much as any mother could love a child. And once Noel had moved in, they'd felt like a family. Dozens of other kids came and went over the years. She'd developed close ties with most of them, but in her heart she'd never felt they really belonged to her. Not the way Meg and Noel did.

Holly thought about the choices that faced her. Phillip had been less than thrilled that she wanted to take time off. He'd argued that the syndication proposal was on the line, and the deal could be killed completely if she wasn't around. She'd considered abandoning her quest for two seconds, until she'd let her heart consider the possibility of a sibling, or even parents. Her goal in life had been to build a fabulous career, but her dream had been a family. Was she willing to sacrifice her goal in pursuit of her dream?

Holly yawned as she finished the last of her drink. The combination of an emotional day and the effect of a martini on an empty stomach left her feeling drowsy and light-headed. She kicked off her shoes and curled into the soft leather beneath her. *Maybe I'll just rest for a minute*, she thought as she felt herself drift away into the realm of exhausted slumber.

Chapter 2

Wednesday November 27

Somewhere around three a.m., Holly woke up and realized she hadn't done anything Ben had told her to do. She needed to pack, notify her landlord of her absence, pay her bills, and have someone water her plants. Stumbling into the shower, she turned it on high and let the pulsating water wash over her body and clear her mind.

A couple of pairs of jeans, a few sweaters, maybe a T-shirt or two, tennis shoes, snow boots, a ski jacket, a knit cap, heavy socks, some changes of underwear, something to sleep in. Holly mentally made a list of the clothes she'd need for a trip of indeterminate length as she shampooed her hair and shaved her legs. Her mind raced to and fro as she conditioned her hair and applied a generous amount of scented body wash to her slender frame.

Holly had always wished for curves, generous curves like Noel had. Instead she was petite, with a boyish figure and total lack of body fat. She'd had nicknames like Peanut and Tink when she was growing up, all the while longing for something sexier.

After drying her five foot one and a quarter inch frame on a large fluffy towel, she brushed her teeth, liberally rubbed in a body lotion that matched the scent of her body wash, and dressed in a faded pair of blue jeans and a soft red sweater. She dried her long blonde hair and applied a light dusting of makeup. Deeming herself presentable, she cleaned up her apartment, watered her plants, paid her bills, penned a note for her landlord, and packed her suitcase. She was just grabbing her red goose-down ski jacket from the hall closet when the doorbell rang.

"You're ready. Good." Ben handed her a tall red cup full of steamy liquid adrenaline.

"Bright and early. Just as you commanded."

"I'll load your stuff and we'll be on our way. We should be able to get out of the city before rush hour really kicks in. Barring any complications or inclement weather, I think we should be able to meet with Mr. Remington on Friday afternoon."

"Friday afternoon?" Holly followed him out of the door. "I mapped our route, and I think we can do much better than that. It's approximately 1430 miles to Fargo," Holly informed him as she followed him down the stairs toward the parking garage. "Once we hit the interstate we should make good time. Allowing for fluctuations in speed due to traffic through the more populated areas, I anticipate an average speed of sixty miles an hour, which should put us in Fargo around this time tomorrow morning."

"What about breaks?" Ben asked as he stowed her luggage in the cargo area of his black Range Rover.

"Breaks? I guess we'll need to stop for fuel, but if we take turns driving, we should still be in Fargo by midmorning."

"Tomorrow is Thanksgiving," Ben pointed out as he closed the door to the cargo area.

"So?" Holly climbed into the passenger seat, adjusted the seat settings, and buckled her seat belt.

"I called the nursing home to find out Mr. Remington's Thanksgiving plans. The attendant I spoke to told me that his son usually picks him up for the day but brings him back Thursday evening. I was told I could call on Friday morning to make an appointment for later that day."

"But that means we'll have to waste a whole day," Holly complained as Ben put the car into reverse and pulled into the back alley.

"How about we just hit the road and see how it goes?" Ben suggested. "Over the years, I've learned that the secret to a successful road trip is to relax and take things as they come. Adapt to your circumstances as you go."

Holly took a deep breath. "So you want me to be that Holly?" she grumbled. "Moosehead Holly. Go-with-the-flow-and-see-how-it-goes Holly."

"If that translates to relaxing and enjoying the journey, then yeah."

"Okay, we'll do it your way. For now," Holly specified, before she turned on her phone and began checking her e-mails.

The drive through the waking city was a quiet one as they both sipped their coffee, lost in their own thoughts. By the time they'd crossed the border from New Jersey into Pennsylvania, it had started to snow. Normally Holly loved the first snow of the season. It was beautiful and refreshing and conjured up happy memories of growing up in Minnesota, sledding with her friends, and building snow forts from which to wage snowball fights with other kids living in the neighborhood.

Today, however, the snow represented an unwanted obstacle to her journey. As she watched the landscape turn white, she felt herself becoming increasingly tense with each passing mile. Twenty-four hours ago, she hadn't even known about the mystery of her birth, but now that she did, finding the truth had taken on an urgency she couldn't quite explain.

What if she had a brother or sister out there? What if she had parents and grandparents, and the huge extended family she'd always wished for? What if they'd mourned her absence from their lives, the way she had always mourned their absence from hers?

"Are you hungry?" Ben broke the silence for the first time.

Was she hungry? Good question. She felt too numb to really tell, but she glanced at the dashboard clock and figured she must be. "Starving," she answered. "In all the excitement, I totally forgot to eat yesterday."

"There's a truck stop with surprisingly good food about a half hour up the road. We'll stop there."

"We could just grab a snack and continue on our way," Holly said.

"I know you're anxious to find your answers." Ben glanced away from the road and momentarily looked directly into her eyes. "I understand. However, we have a long journey ahead of us, and I for one am going to need to stretch my legs."

"Yeah, I guess you're right." Holly knew she needed a distraction. They'd only been on the road for a few hours and already she felt like she was on the verge of jumping out of her skin. Her boss had agreed to a ten-day leave of absence. And beyond that? Beyond that, she'd have to make choices. Choices she'd prefer not to have to make.

She took a deep breath and willed herself to relax. To enjoy the scenery. "I guess I should call Jessica and check in anyway. She should be in the office by the time we stop. They'll close at noon today for the long holiday weekend, but since I didn't finish my column before I left as I'd planned, I'll need to finish it and send it to her by Friday."

"Will you be working while we're away?" Ben asked.

"I'm always working," Holly replied. "My assistant, Jessica, is going to read my mail and scan and e-mail the top five or six letters every day. She does a lot of my research anyway, so I'll just need to make certain to reserve a few hours to actually write my replies."

"So you're an advice columnist?"

"Sort of. Women write in with problems, and I try to offer them both advice and practical solutions," Holly explained. "Most problems have both a practical and emotional or psychological component to them."

"Such as?"

"About a year ago, I had a woman write in at the edge of her rope because she didn't know how to deal with her ninety-year-old grandmother. It seems the grandmother was a feisty old gal who had lived on her own since the girl's grandfather had died forty years earlier. Her problem was that the grandmother had been experiencing some health issues; nothing life threatening, but enough so that she couldn't really take care of herself any longer. The granddaughter had been trying to stop by on a daily basis to take care of the cooking, cleaning, errands, and whatnot, but she had her own job and her own family and was completely worn out."

"Sounds like an assisted-care facility would be the answer," Ben suggested.

"It would seem so, but the family didn't have the money to move her into a private facility, and the grandmother said she'd rather die than go to a public one."

"I guess I can understand that," Ben sympathized. "So what advice did you give her?"

"I found out that the state where the woman lived had a fantastic home-aide system. Not only would someone come to the grandmother's home every day and see to the cooking, cleaning, bathing, and errands, but the program was free. The problem was, Grandma didn't want some stranger coming around every day so, when offered, she turned the program down."

"I'm assuming you eventually got the old girl to go along with the plan?"

"I did, but it wasn't easy. I knew I had to find a hook the grandmother couldn't refute. I had a long talk with the granddaughter and found out that the grandma had been spending almost her entire social security check on prescription drugs, so when I realized that the program I found subsidized the cost of prescriptions for all participants who qualified, I realized I had my hook."

"So Grandma was persuaded to take the help in the home in order to get help with her prescriptions," Ben guessed.

"Exactly. She complained a lot at first, but every time she threatened not to let her caregiver help out, the granddaughter just needed to remind her that the help with the prescriptions came as part of a package deal. Eventually, the woman relaxed and actually became friends with the helper who came by every day."

"Sounds like you really helped that family."

"I believe I did, and others as well. As part of my published response to the letter, I listed the states that provided this type of service and gave contact information for anyone who might qualify. I believe my column educates people about services that are available that they might not know about. Jessica is a genius on the computer and can find pretty much anything if it exists. Coupled with my degree in journalism, we make a pretty effective team. I really love what I do."

Ben smiled. "It shows."

"How about you?" Holly asked. "Do you have work to take care of while we're gone?"

"No," Ben replied. "I'm pretty much freelance, so you have my undivided attention for the entire month."

Holly glanced at the broad chest covered by a soft blue sweater and let her imagination run wild just for a moment. She didn't have time for a relationship, but every now and then she fantasized about finding just the right man. Ben definitely had potential. Not only was he gorgeous, but so far he appeared to be kind and attentive, *and* they were going to be spending a lot of time alone with each other over the next few weeks. This would be a perfect opportunity to get to know the man Aunt Meg had trusted enough to help her find the answers to her past.

"So Ben Holiday," Holly turned slightly in her seat so she was facing him, "you know a lot about me, but I know absolutely nothing about you."

"What do you want to know?"

What she really wanted to know, she realized, was whether he was single, and whether he found himself attracted to her the way she was attracted to him. She wondered whether he knew that the sweater he wore matched his eyes exactly, or if he realized how the dark hair covering strong hands as they gripped the wheel of the vehicle caused butterflies in her stomach that she couldn't totally attribute to nerves.

"Well, for starters," she said instead, "how do you know Aunt Meg, why were you playing poker with her, and if you weren't out of money, why did you bet yourself in the first place?"

"Direct and to the point. I like that." Ben smiled. "In answer to your first question, I bought a house out at Beaver Lake a couple of years ago, and I met Meg at church. She was in charge of the annual Christmas pageant, and I offered to help out building sets."

Holly knew that Beaver Lake was just north of her hometown of Moosehead. While the north shore of the lake was populated by seasonal cabins, there were a few full-time residents living on the south shore, where a privately owned road provided year-round access into town.

"Church? Really? You don't look like the type to go to church."

"You have to look a certain way to go to church?"

"Well, no. It's just that Meg used to drag me to church every Sunday, and I don't remember anyone there who was quite so . . ." *gorgeous* "single."

"How do you know I'm single?"

"You're not?" Holly's heart skipped a beat.

"I am, but I don't remember telling you that. For all you know, I could have a wife and four kids back at the lake."

Holly stopped to consider that. "If you had a wife and four kids, you wouldn't be taking off on a road trip across the country with me."

"True," Ben acknowledged. "In answer to your second question, I was playing poker with Meg because Jordy Miller passed away last year and Meg invited me to join the Tuesday morning poker group in his place."

"You're kidding. There can't be a single person under sixty-five in that group."

"Actually, I think the youngest person next to me is Rupert Palmer, and he's seventy-two. But I find the group to be both well versed and entertaining. Most of the members have lived in Moosehead most, if not all, of their lives. They're full of colorful stories about the town's history. And, of course, they're up on all the local gossip. It's quite educational. You should join us sometime."

"I don't know." Holly hesitated. "They're pretty picky about who they let into their exclusive little group. They might not want me."

"Are you kidding? Everyone in town loves you. Many a Tuesday morning has been spent discussing Holly Thompson and her colorful past."

"Please tell me you're lying." Holly cringed.

"Sorry," Ben smiled, "but you're going to get talked about if, as a kid, you poured oil on the floor of the elementary-school hallways and then pulled the fire alarm so that everyone was slipping and sliding as they tried to get out. Or if you painted the words *help me* and *eat chicken* in bright red paint on the side of the Wilsons' prize cows right before the county fair. Or if you decided to go skinny-dipping in Old Man Johnson's pond with half the senior class looking on. That was my favorite story of all, by the way."

Holly buried her head in her arms as Ben finished speaking. "I can't believe they told you all of that."

"That and a lot more. Shall I go on?"

"God, no." Holly thought for certain she'd die of embarrassment. Growing up, she'd never felt like she really belonged, though she'd tried really hard to fit in. And, unfortunately, the group she most wanted to fit in with was an older and slightly deviant crowd that one of her foster brothers introduced her to. Poor Meg had had her hands full during Holly's rebellious stage, which had lasted most of her childhood.

"You must think I'm a complete idiot," she said, groaning.

"Actually, I found the stories to be both charming and endearing. Which leads me to the third part of your question: why I bet myself instead of money. Meg and I got to be close friends during the two years I knew her, and we shared many a heartfelt talk. I knew Meg felt bad about not telling you the entire story about your past, and I knew that she was greatly concerned about how the news would affect you. She was aware that she was dying, and it haunted her that you'd have to deal with all of this without support. I knew it would be important to you to find your answers, and I wanted to help, but Meg would never take charity, so on the particular Tuesday in question, I found my opportunity and took it."

Holly waited for him to continue as he slowed the vehicle and turned up the windshield wipers. The snow had increased in intensity, causing the scenery outside the window to fade into the whiteness. Ben pulled into the slow lane behind an eighteen-wheel truck and continued with his story.

"There was a point when just Meg and I were left in a hotly contested game. She had a great hand, which was obvious to everyone because she was much too open and honest to have a believable poker face. Everyone else folded, so I threw away four kings and pretended I was out of money but offered my services in exchange. She accepted the bet, and the rest is history."

"Wow. That was so nice." Holly stared at the taillights in front of her and willed herself not to cry. By this point in her life, she should have been used to people being nice to her for no apparent reason, but somehow she really wasn't. "Thank you. I mean, really. How can I ever repay you?"

"There's no need to repay me. I wanted to do this. I was glad to have the opportunity to ease Meg's mind, and I was looking forward to having the chance to get to know the famous Holly Thompson."

"Really?"

"Really." He winked and melted her heart just a bit. "We're almost to the truck stop. They have excellent omelets, if you like eggs. My favorite is the bacon, cheese, and mushroom."

"Sounds heavy."

"Eat up. I thought we'd drive straight through till dinner. We should be in Toledo around seven, and we can stop there to get a bite to eat and then decide if we want to stay there for the night or continue on for a few more hours."

By the time they reached the outskirts of Toledo, the snow was coming down harder than ever, and a flashing sign on the highway informed motorists that the road was closed ahead due to an overturned tanker. Ben slowed to a stop and shifted the Range Rover into park. Turning down the heater, he let the vehicle idle while he pulled up current road conditions on his phone. According to the traffic control website, there wasn't yet an anticipated time for the road to reopen.

"We have two choices," Ben informed her as she stared at the long line of cars ahead of them. "We can get off here and look for a motel, or we can double back approximately ten miles and catch US 6 west. It's a pretty good road, but in this snow I'm not sure."

"Let's try US 6," Holly said. "That four-hour nap I took after breakfast has left me feeling energetic and wide awake. By the way, I'm sorry about that. I'm not being a very good road-trip companion. I hope I didn't snore."

"No, but you mumbled a little."

"Oh God. What did I say?"

"Don't worry, nothing too embarrassing." Ben grinned in a manner that suggested otherwise. "Once we finally get off the interstate, it should be a quick trip back to US 6. We'll try it out, and if the road's too bad, we'll find a motel and wait out the storm. There are several small towns along the route."

Holly looked at the long line of taillights waiting to exit. "It's going to take an hour just to get turned around."

"Probably. Want to listen to the radio?"

"Actually, since we're just sitting still and you don't really have to focus on your driving, I'd like to ask you about what else you uncovered in your investigation. Yesterday, when you told me about John Remington, you said you found out several things. I have to admit I'm curious about what those other things might be."

"Are you sure you want to talk about this now?" Ben asked. "In spite of your nap, you look exhausted. Listening to a few holiday tunes would be less intense."

Holly wasn't sure how things could get any more intense than they already were. "I'm sure. I want—no, I *need* to know."

"Okay." Ben shifted the car into drive and inched forward with the rest of the stranded motorists. "The first thing I did after identifying and locating Mr. Remington was put a trace on the car in which you were found. It was registered to a Carl Langley of Gardiner, Montana, a small town just outside of Yellowstone National Park. I did some checking and found out that Mr. Langley passed away in his home, most likely a day or so before the automobile accident you were involved in, although since the body wasn't found for several days, they never did determine an exact time of death."

"Before the accident?" Holly asked. "How did he die?"

"The police investigated and ruled it a death by natural causes, but the timing seems a little suspicious to me. The police were never able to verify how the couple driving the car came to have it in their possession. Did Mr. Langley lend it to them? Did they steal it? There are a lot of unanswered questions, but no real leads. I did verify that Mr. Langley never reported the car stolen, so he either lent it to them or they stole it after his death."

"Did anyone from town remember anything?" Holly wondered.

"No," Ben confirmed. "I'm not sure how hard the local police tried to turn over rocks, but the report I saw said that Mr. Langley was a recluse who lived outside of the incorporated area on a large piece of property and rarely came into town."

It sounded like another dead end. "So how can we follow up on that?" Holly asked.

"I figured we'd head to Gardiner after we speak to Mr. Remington, unless he gives us a better lead to follow up on. After twenty-seven years, I'm not sure we'll have any better luck putting the pieces of the puzzle together than the police who first investigated the incident did, but it couldn't hurt to try."

"Anything else?" Holly asked hopefully.

"The police report I managed to acquire stated that both of the diaper bags that were recovered contained infant-size clothing for a girl."

"So I have a sister?"

"Possibly," Ben concurred. "It occurred to me that since both bags contained the same size clothing, the two babies, if there were two babies, must have been twins."

"Twins. Do you realize there might be someone out there who looks just like me?"

"The thought occurred to me, so I borrowed a photo from Meg and sent it to a buddy who works at the FBI. He's going to see if he can find a match in any of their facial recognition programs. I also did a search of all the twins born during the week prior to the accident within a 500-mile radius. It took a while, but I've managed to verify the whereabouts of all the names I came up with. None of them are missing sisters or look like you. At this point, I'm going with the original investigator's assessment that you were born outside of the hospital system."

"Wow, you were busy." Holly wasn't sure how she felt about the fact that Ben had apparently known for months about the mystery surrounding her birth but was only now telling her about it. She supposed he wanted to get a baseline of information from which to begin their search, but still, it was her life. Shouldn't she have been part of the initial search?

"By the way," she said, "how do you happen to know someone from the FBI, and how did you get your hands on all of those police records?"

"I used to be a New York City police officer, but I left the force two years ago. I also did a stint in DC when I first started out. I'm a nice guy." He shrugged. "I made a lot of friends."

"Why did you quit?"

"I was injured in a bust in which my partner and best friend Steven, and my eldest sister, Peg, were both killed."

"Oh, I'm so sorry."

"It was the darkest time of my life, even worse than when my father was killed. After the incident, my mom begged me to quit the force and do something safer. I come from a long line of cops: my grandfather, uncles, even my dad. My dad died flying home from a fishing trip, but my Uncle Bob died in the line of duty, just like Peg."

"So you quit for your mom? Was it a hard decision?"

"It was, at least at first." Ben shrugged again. "My whole life, I always assumed I'd be a cop. I don't remember ever wanting to do anything else. Being a cop was a huge part of my self-identity. If I wasn't a cop, who was I? I loved my job, but I love my mom more, and when I saw the depth of despair on her face at my sister's funeral, I agreed to quit. She had already lost a brother and a daughter to the force. I knew she couldn't bear to lose a son. So I quit and became a private investigator."

"Do you miss it? Being on the force?"

"Surprisingly, no. I thought I would. But I found out that being a private investigator is rewarding. I'm able to pick and choose my cases, and I've been able to help a lot of people find the answers they needed."

"Why move to Beaver Lake?" Holly asked as Ben merged onto the off ramp. "There can't be much work for a private investigator in sleepy little Moosehead."

"I knew if I stayed in New York, I'd feel like I was living on the fringe of my old life. I needed a complete change. My dad used to take me fishing at Beaver Lake, and I have a lot of great memories of the place. When I found a house for sale just across the lake from where we used to fish, I bought it. I can really live anywhere. I have a lot of connections, and with them come a ton of referrals. I accept the ones I want to and politely decline the others. I'm not really into the tailing-a-cheating-spouse gigs."

Holly supposed being a private investigator would be interesting. At least the books and movies made it seem so. When she was in the fourth grade, she and Noel had formed a Nancy Drew club, of which Noel had been the president and she'd been the vice president. It all started when Mrs. Wilson lost her cat, and she and Noel followed the clues, which led to his rescue from one of the kids in the neighborhood, who had locked the poor thing in his tree house.

After the success of that investigation, the pair had been hooked and spent most of their combined savings on "spy ware" they'd found in a mail-order catalogue. Holly had to admit that most of their investigating that summer was little more than spying, but it had been fun while it lasted.

"What kind of cases have you taken on in the past two years?"

Ben seemed to pause to consider her question "Last year I found the five-year-old daughter of a banking executive. She'd been kidnapped and was being held for ransom. That case was particularly rewarding, since I have six nieces myself, and I couldn't imagine how I'd feel if one of them was being held against her will."

"Wow. How long was she missing?"

"Five days. I'm sure the longest of her poor parents' lives. Luckily, the kidnappers were just after money and treated her well. She was scared, but there wasn't a scratch on her when I finally tracked her down at an abandoned warehouse less than five miles from where she was taken."

"Really? Five miles . . . and the local police couldn't find her?"

"No. The kidnappers had her hidden pretty well. They were smart enough not to try to transport her over any great distance. They would have run a much greater risk of being caught on the road."

Holly could only imagine how fantastic it must have been to reunite a small child with her frightened parents. She could remember how awesome it had felt to reunite Mrs. Wilson with her missing cat. Being a private investigator sounded like the coolest job on earth. Well, next to hers, that is.

"What else?" she asked.

"I helped a couple in Chicago find their runaway daughter. She was in Los Angeles, living on the street and trying to become the next big thing. It was really a pretty easy case because she was more than ready to come home by the time I located her."

Maybe it was no big deal to him, but Holly imagined it was probably a huge deal to the girls' parents.

"What's been your hardest case so far?"

Ben's smile faded a bit as he thought. "I helped a family investigate the disappearance of their adult son. He was twenty-two and fresh out of college. Unfortunately, that one didn't end so well. My investigation led to the discovery of his body and the facts surrounding his rather gruesome murder. He went to a party and never came home, and for three years his parents had no idea what had happened to him. They were understandably upset when they found out the truth, but at least they could bury him and get some closure."

"It must be awful to have a missing child and never know what happened to them. I can't imagine anything worse. You know . . ." Holly hesitated. "It just occurred to me…"

"That if the woman in the car wasn't your biological mother, you might have been kidnapped by the couple who perished in the accident," Ben finished.

"How did you know?"

"It occurred to me, too."

"Do you think that's what happened? Do you think I have parents out there who never knew what happened to me?"

"Maybe. I don't know. I promise you, though, I'll do everything in my power to help you find out."

The cars ahead of them started to move, so Ben refocused his attention on the road while Holly snuggled down in her seat and leaned her head against the window, staring out at the swirling snow. On one hand, she needed to know the answer to this increasingly complicated puzzle; on the other, she was terrified of what she might find out.

The snow had let up by the time they made it back to US 6, so they decided to drive for a couple of hours before stopping for the night. Ben turned the radio to a station that played soft jazz as they drove into the darkening horizon. Alone with her thoughts, Holly tried to make sense of everything she'd learned so far. Was it possible that she had been kidnapped as an infant? Was there a family out there that had been looking for her all these years? And if so, why hadn't they ever reported her missing? Surely if a police case had been opened, they would have discovered her identity a long time ago.

Maybe her parents were dead. Or maybe they hadn't wanted a child and had given her to the couple she was with the night of the accident. Ben had said they hadn't been able to find a record of her birth. Was it possible that she was one of those abandoned babies left to die in a public bathroom or a Dumpster? Maybe the couple she'd been with had found her on the edge of death and had actually rescued her.

Of course, that didn't explain the second diaper bag and car seat. And would a mom who would abandon her child in a Dumpster buy a diaper bag full of baby clothes? She tried to imagine what might have happened. The entire thing didn't make any sense, no matter how Holly looked at it.

"There's a motel I've stayed at before up ahead on the right, with a café just down the road. What do you say we stop there?" Ben interrupted her troubled thoughts.

"Sounds good." Holly returned her attention to the present. "I can't believe how tired I am after my long nap this afternoon."

"Stress can do that to you. Let's check in first, then walk down the road for dinner. I need to stretch my legs after driving all day."

Holly looked out of the passenger window. The snow had stopped during the past hour, and it looked like a snowplow had been through recently to clear the street. The trees lining the narrow road were heavy with snow, making the area look like a winter wonderland. At home in New York, Holly avoided spending any more time outdoors in the snow than was absolutely necessary, meaning her taxi budget doubled during the winter months. Tonight, however, a brisk walk in the cold night air would be just what she needed to calm her mind so that she'd be able to sleep.

Ben got two rooms with a connecting door. Holly tossed her suitcase on the bed and looked around her room. Modest, but adequate. A queen-size bed, adjoining bath, and old but working television. Maybe she'd pick up a bottle of wine and watch an old movie after she finished her column, which, thanks to Jessica, was all but done. Holly had a suspicion that falling peacefully to sleep was going to be a bit of a challenge with the very distracting Ben on the other side of what appeared to be very thin walls.

After digging out her red knit cap and mittens, Holly bundled into her down jacket and snow boots and set off walking down the road with Ben.

"It's freezing out here, but it's really pretty with all the fresh snow reflecting the lights," Holly commented. "The magic of a winter night after a fresh snow is one of the things I really miss about Moosehead. When I was a little girl, I used to like to find a patch of snow that no one else had walked on and make snow angels."

Ben smiled. "I can totally picture you as a little girl. I bet you were adorable."

"Of course." Holly opened the door to the diner and slipped her hat and gloves into the pockets of her jacket.

"Sit anywhere you like," the middle-aged waitress told them.

Holly slid into a booth next to the window and took off her jacket. The bushes outside the window were covered in white twinkling lights, giving the landscape a magical feel. She hadn't expected to enjoy the holidays at all this year, but all of a sudden she found herself with the warm glow she'd enjoyed as a child.

"Soup's broccoli cheese, special's meatloaf, and pies are cherry and pumpkin." The waitress set glasses of water and handwritten menus in front of them. "Everything on the menu is available, but I wouldn't recommend the tenderloin. Cook got it overdone today. Had a piece for lunch and it wasn't tender at all. Can I get you anything else to drink while you look over the menu?"

"Water's fine, thanks." Holly smiled at the tired-looking woman.

"I'll have coffee," Ben answered.

"This late? You'll be awake all night," Holly whispered as the waitress walked away to get their drinks.

"I didn't get a lot of sleep last night. A tankard of coffee couldn't keep me awake."

Lucky him. "How come you couldn't sleep?"

Ben leaned across the table and tucked a stray lock of hair behind Holly's ear. He looked into her eyes and ran his finger along her jaw. "I had a lot on my mind."

Holly held her breath as he caressed her cheek with his thumb several times before dropping his hand and looking toward the waitress, who returned with their drinks and took their order. Holly wanted to ask if he had the same thing on his mind as she had on hers, but said instead, "So if you've lived in Moosehead for two years, how come I've never seen you there?"

"Maybe you have." He took a sip of his coffee. "You wouldn't necessarily remember seeing me if you didn't know who I was."

"Oh, I'd remember." Holly was certain that if she'd spotted Ben, even across a crowded store or restaurant, she'd remember him. She'd never met anyone who was put together so absolutely perfectly as the man across from her appeared to be.

"Maybe I happened to be on a case or holed up at the lake doing research when you were there," Ben suggested. "There are often long stretches of time when I don't come into town."

"Maybe," Holly conceded. "But if you were such great friends with Meg, why weren't you at her funeral?'

"I was. I stayed toward the back, but I was there. You looked so lost I wanted to comfort you, but since you didn't know me from Adam, I decided to keep my distance."

Holly looked at him skeptically.

"You had on a black suit with a belt that tied around the waist. You wore your hair down and I couldn't help but notice how it fell across your face as you read the eulogy, which was beautiful, by the way. It occurred to me that perhaps you'd worn your hair down intentionally so as to have something to hide behind if the need presented itself. Need I go on?"

"No, that's okay. But say that's true . . ." Holly sat back in the booth and realized that perhaps she should have asked this type of question before heading off across the country with a man she'd just met and didn't really know anything about. What proof did she have that Ben was who he said he was? "In two years' time, why didn't Meg ever mention you? For that matter, why didn't Noel? Noel has tried to throw me at every even remotely eligible guy in Moosehead, yet she didn't even mention you. Somehow that doesn't track."

Holly waited for him to explain his way out of that one. The guy could be a con artist who'd stolen Meg's tape to get her to . . . to what? She was being ridiculous. What possible reason could he have to drag her across the country other than the one he had already given her?

"Noel doesn't like me," Ben answered.

"What do you mean, she doesn't like you? Noel likes everyone. Well, everyone except Donny Preston's new wife, apparently." When she'd spoken to Noel the previous morning, she'd explained that their old friend Donny Preston was in town with his new wife, who apparently had been ruffling feathers all over town. A trust-fund baby with more money than Midas, she seemed to think that every citizen in the quaint little town in which her new husband had grown up existed for no other reason than to bow to her every whim.

"When I first came to town, I was introduced to her husband Tommy by a mutual acquaintance," Ben explained. "We stopped by the Watering Hole for a friendly drink, but one thing led to another and Tommy got totally wasted. By the time Noel wandered into town looking for her missing husband, a couple of attractive women who were traveling through town on business had joined us. Needless to say, Noel was furious. She blames me for the whole thing. According to her, I'm a bad influence."

"Wow, poor Noel. I can see why she'd feel that way. To be honest, I'm kind of surprised Tommy would do something like that."

"I don't think he meant to," Ben defended him. "Noel had just had the newest baby in the ever-growing Davis clan, and I think Tommy and Noel were both seriously sleep deprived. I can't even begin to imagine how exhausting a new baby must be when you already have three children. The law firm Tommy works for had just lost a big case that day, one that Tommy had worked on almost exclusively. When Larry, our mutual friend, suggested that the three of us stop off for a drink, Tommy was all for it."

So far what Ben was saying made sense.

"Unfortunately, one drink turned into three and then four, and before we knew it, Tommy was totally hammered. Larry left before Noel arrived, so I looked like the sole instigator. As for the women, they just sat down with us. We didn't invite them over. They'd only been sitting with us for a few minutes when Noel showed up."

"Did you try explaining all of this to Noel?"

"No. Tommy was in a heap of trouble, so I decided to take the blame for the incident. It was really no sweat off me. I didn't know her then, but now that I know she's your best friend, I guess I'll have to try to mend a few fences."

Holly smiled. He talked as if their friendship would continue after their adventure ended. "Don't worry. Noel has a legendary temper, but she also has a kind heart. I'm sure she'll give you a second chance. I'll just have to figure out a way of clearing your name without making Tommy look any worse. How about this Larry guy? Any chance we could make him the scapegoat?"

"No, Larry and Tommy are friends. I wouldn't want to mess that up. We'll have to figure out another way."

The waitress set steaming plates of meatloaf, mashed potatoes, green beans, and gravy before each of them, ending the conversation.

After they'd finished the carb-heavy meal, they waddled back to the hotel and went straight to their respective rooms after agreeing to meet at eight o'clock in the morning for breakfast.

Chapter 3

Thursday, November 28

By morning, the snow had stopped and the plows had been through, so the drive to Fargo was smooth and uneventful. Holly decided to use the time to catch up on some of the work she had promised to do while she was away. Normally, the time between receiving a letter and actually publishing a response was about a month. When the mail arrived each day, Jessica opened it, read the letters, then set a few on the top of the pile. The letters chosen made it onto a list of possibilities. From the list of candidates, Holly chose between three and five to have Jessica research. Of those, maybe two were published in the magazine, while several others made the blog, which she tried to update every day.

When possible, all the letters Holly received were answered in one way or another by either herself or Jessica. A fair number required nothing more than a gentle nudge to convince her readers to do what they already seemed to know they should do. Still others were outside her realm of expertise, so her answer was little more than contact information for someone who could better assist the letter writer.

"Anything interesting?" Ben asked after they had been driving quietly for a few hours.

"They're all interesting, but yeah, there were a couple of good one's in this week's mail. Seems the holiday season brings out both the crazy and the desperation in people. This is the fourth letter I've read today in which a parent is asking if I have an in with a toy company because they can't find the must-have toy of the year."

"Do you," Ben said, "have an in with toy companies?"

"No, I'm afraid I don't. Not really, that is. But sometimes a phone call letting the right person know that I'm writing a human-interest story about the heart behind the toy empire has netted the desired toy."

"You'd go to all that trouble for a toy?"

"Well, not every time. But many of the parents who write have a compelling reason for wanting to make sure their little darling has the perfect toy on Christmas morning. A sick child or one who has just lost a loved one. Last year I managed to track down the *it* doll for a little girl whose mom had just passed away after a long illness. I called the toy company and convinced them it was a win/win situation: I'd write an article about the soul behind the conglomerate, making them look like kindhearted elves, and the little girl would get the doll she swore her mom had promised Santa would bring her before she died, possibly making all the difference in what promised to be a difficult holiday for both the little girl and her father."

"That was really a nice thing to do." Ben smiled.

Holly shrugged. "Not nice; just my job."

"So would it be a betrayal of confidence to read me some of those letters?" Ben asked. "It's been a long drive."

"I can read them. No one uses their real name anyway."

Holly spent the next hour reading some of her newest submissions and discussing with him possible answers to the questions. Like Jessica, Ben had a lot of good ideas and insights into what the best possible solution to a particular circumstance might be. The lively discussion helped to pass the time, and before they knew it, they were pulling into the outskirts of Fargo.

After arriving in town and checking into a motel, Ben and Holly decided to splurge and enjoy a Thanksgiving dinner at the nicest restaurant they could find. There weren't a lot of restaurants near the motel to choose from, but they found one that was offering a "home- cooked" Thanksgiving special.

"It seems so strange to be eating Thanksgiving dinner in a restaurant," Holly commented as a waitress set plates of turkey, stuffing, mashed potatoes and gravy, cranberries, green beans, and freshly baked rolls in front of them. "I always celebrated Thanksgiving with Aunt Meg. She was a genius in the kitchen. Her pecan pies are legendary. And her stuffing . . . I really miss her."

"I know. Me, too."

"How about you?" Holly asked. "Do you usually have Thanksgiving with your family?"

"Yeah, every year until last year. I just couldn't work up the enthusiasm I usually have for the holidays after my sister died, so I called my mom and made up some lame excuse. At the time, it seemed like the best thing to do, but in retrospect I guess it was pretty selfish not to go home. I'm sure my mom was missing Peg as much as I was. I told myself that she had Marty, and my sisters and nieces, but if I'm totally honest, I'm sure she really missed having me home. I'm going to make a point to go home for Christmas this year."

"Marty?"

"The man she married after my dad died. He's really great. You'll like him. He has a real sense of humor."

"I'll be meeting him?"

"I'm sure you will. By the time we finish this investigation, whatever the outcome, I'm sure we'll be fast friends. At least I hope we will."

Holly smiled.

"So how come you aren't having turkey with your family right now?" Holly wondered. "Our trip could have waited another couple of days."

"My mom went to my eldest sister's husband's parents' house for the holiday," he answered. "My sisters usually trade off having Christmas and Thanksgiving with their respective husbands' families, and one or another of them usually invites my mom and Marty. There have been a few times when Mom, Marty, and I have had our own dinner, but since I wanted to get started on our trip, I told them I'd pass on Thanksgiving this year but try to make it home for Christmas. How about you? Did you have plans if I hadn't shown up?"

"I was having dinner with my imaginary boyfriend." Holly explained about her conversation with Noel, and how she'd made up a date to put Noel's mind at ease.

Ben laughed at her impersonation of a fake boyfriend with a really bad English accent who she'd made up in her mind in order to describe him to Noel when she called.

"Maybe we should bundle up and take a walk after dinner to work off all this food," Ben suggested.

"Sounds good. Between last night's dinner and tonight's, I think I'm about to go into carb overload."

After paying the bill, they headed back to the motel to get heavy jackets, snow boots, hats, and gloves. It couldn't be more than ten degrees, but after two long days of sitting for hours on end in the car, Holly couldn't wait to set off down the street toward a park they had seen when they drove into town.

"Unmarred snow," Ben commented. "How about we see some of those famous snow angels you were bragging about?"

"You're on." Holly flopped down onto her back and began moving her arms and legs back and forth. "Now the secret is to get up without ruining it. Give me a hand."

Ben reached down and pulled Holly out of the snow and into his arms.

"Th . . . thanks," Holly stuttered as Ben gently wiped snow from her face.

Ben leaned forward as if he was going to kiss her, thought better of it, then pulled away and took a step back. "You were right. You do make excellent snow angels. There's a path that runs along the lake; how about we try that?"

"Okay," Holly almost choked. Willing her heartbeat to slow, she turned and let Ben lead her toward the path.

"Ben?" Holly asked as they walked hand in hand along the lake path. "Are you seeing anyone? Romantically, I mean. Like a girlfriend or maybe a fiancée?"

"No. Why?"

"Just curious."

"How about you?" Ben asked. "Any attachments I should know about?"

"No. I'm attachment free. Well, except for my pretend boyfriend Noel thinks I'm having dinner with at this very moment. It's not that I couldn't get a real boyfriend if I wanted one," she qualified. "It's just that I've been really busy, and ever since Meg first got sick, I just haven't been in a romantic frame of mind." Holly picked up a clump of snow and molded it into a ball. "Sorry. I'm rambling. I do that when I get nervous."

"Are you nervous?" Ben stopped walking and turned to face her, with only inches between them.

"Intensely," she whispered, her breath mingling with his.

"Why?" He leaned in just a touch.

"Because," she spoke very softly, very seductively, "I'm afraid," she whispered, her lips less than an inch from his, "you might get mad when I stuff this snowball down your jacket." Which she proceeded to do before running off down the path and out of harm's way.

"Why you little . . ." Ben laughed before taking off down the path after her. "You are in so much trouble. Just wait until I catch you," he yelled from behind her.

Ben fashioned a snowball and threw it at Holly, hitting her squarely in the middle of the back. She laughed and returned fire with her own hastily made ammunition. Hiding behind a clump of bushes, Ben hastily molded his own artillery and the war was on.

"Okay, okay, I give," Holly yelled fifteen minutes later as she brushed snow from her hair and jacket.

Ben snuck up behind her and wrapped his arms around her, pinning her arms to her sides. "Not so fast. I think I owe you a snowball down your jacket."

"No, please." Holly laughed. "I'm freezing. I'll probably catch pneumonia, and then you'll have to spend the next week nursing me back to health."

"Huh?" Ben pretended to be contemplating his options. "The idea has possibilities."

"Ben!" Holly twisted around so that her arms were still pinned but they stood face-to-face. "Pneumonia is a serious thing. People die from it."

"Then I guess we'd better get you warmed up."

Ben released Holly's arms and cupped her face with his glove-encased hands. He looked directly into her eyes before he slowly leaned forward and gently touched her cold lips with his own. All too quickly, Ben lifted his head and looked deeply into her eyes once again.

"Warmer?"

Holly couldn't speak; she simply nodded her head as Ben put his arm around her and started to walk back toward the motel. When they got to her room, he took the key from her shaking hand and opened her door.

"Feel free to sleep in. I called the nursing home after we got to the motel. We're not meeting with John Remington until eleven o'clock."

Holly simply stared at him, as if she couldn't quite form a coherent thought.

"Sweet dreams." He kissed her on the forehead, ushered her into her room, and unlocked his own room next door.

Holly stood staring at the wall in front of her for several minutes before she sat down on the corner of the bed and pulled off her wet hat and gloves.

She was at a total loss as to what to make of what had just happened. Ben had kissed her in a way that made the world sort of fade away, and then he had acted like nothing momentous had happened. Maybe it was just her? Maybe Ben experienced earth-shattering kisses every day? Worse yet, maybe he hadn't felt the earth move the way she had. Maybe to Ben their kiss was just one among many.

Holly began to shake as the cold seeped back into her body. She numbly slithered out of her wet jacket and stumbled her way into the bathroom, where she ran a bath as hot as her frozen skin could stand.

Sliding into the steaming water, she leaned back and rested her head against the rim of the tub. She closed her eyes and replayed the kiss over and over again in her mind. He had to have felt something. There was no way she could have felt the way she did if he had felt nothing at all. Maybe he was as stunned as she was. Maybe he was just being polite: a gentleman, controlling the situation. Maybe her lips were cold and clammy and he felt like he was kissing a wet fish. Maybe he could tell how inexperienced she actually was and was appalled.

Oh God. Holly slid deeper into the quickly cooling water. How would she face him the next day? Ben was probably in his room right now trying to figure out how he could take her home without breaking his promise to Meg.

After drying her hair and snuggling into her flannel pajamas, Holly curled up under the covers and called Noel.

"Tell me everything." Noel yawned as she picked up the phone on the first ring.

"How did you know it was me?"

"Who else would be calling me in the middle of the night? Now spill. How was your date?"

"It was . . . nice."

"Nice as in 'I ate way too much turkey,' or nice as in 'it was the most romantic night of my life'?"

"Both, actually."

"Oh, wow. Tell me everything. What's his name?"

"Ben." Holly couldn't help but smile.

"Ben. Sounds nice. What does he look like?"

"Tall, dark hair, the bluest eyes you've ever seen. And he has the most precious smile, sort of lopsided and endearing. And his body is . . . wow. He must work out almost every day. And he has the best hands."

"Hands?" Noel whispered, careful not to wake her sleeping family.

"Strong hands. Hands that would support you and not let you down."

"He sounds perfect. And he can cook?"

"Actually, we went out. It was a very nice restaurant, though, and we had a traditional turkey dinner. And afterward we took a long walk in the park. It was so romantic."

"Are you crazy?" Noel scolded, a little louder than she should have, considering Tommy was sleeping next to her. "You shouldn't be out walking around in Central Park in the middle of the night. You're going to get yourself killed."

Of course. Noel thought she was still in New York. "We were fine. Ben used to be a cop. He knows how to take care of himself."

"Used to be a cop? What is he now?"

"A private investigator."

"Really?" Noel sounded surprised. "I wouldn't have pegged that to be your type at all. I figured for sure that you'd tell me he was a stockbroker or the CEO of a large corporation. How'd you meet?"

"That's a long story and it's really late. I should get to bed."

"Oh no you don't. You haven't even gotten to the good part yet."

"Good part?"

"Yeah, the part that happened after your very romantic stroll in the park."

"He walked me home and I came in and took a bath."

"That's it?"

"That's it."

"You want me to believe you spent the whole evening with this total hunk and nothing happened?"

"Sorry to ruin your vicarious fantasy, but we're just getting to know each other." Holly yawned. "So how was your day?"

"Really nice," Noel purred. "Tommy's brother and his family are in town, so I made a huge family brunch. You'll never believe how big the kids have gotten since the last time they were in town. Lonnie must have grown a foot, and Annabelle is developing into such a beautiful young woman."

"I'm sorry I missed them. Did Tommy's parents come as well?"

"Yeah, and his cousin Vicki came with them."

"How was it?" Holly knew that Noel and Vicki didn't always get along.

"Okay, I guess. She hooked up with Jerry Conner at the community dinner, so at least she won't be coming tree cutting with the rest of us."

"Jerry? I thought he was engaged."

"He was. Guess it didn't work out. Tree lighting is next Friday," Noel informed her. "The town is doing a Victorian Christmas theme this year. There's a decorating party on Monday, and a lot of the retailers are dressing up in vintage costumes. It'd be fun if you could come out for the weekend. You could bring your Ben. The guys could watch football and we could go into the Cities and do some shopping."

"It sounds fun, but I don't think it'll work out this year." Holly glanced at the clock. "I really need to get to bed. I'm exhausted. I'll call you in a day or two."

"Okay." Noel sighed. "There's just one more thing: I ran into Madison Wellington today. She wanted your phone number. I guess she has someone interested in buying the farm."

Holly knew that Madison was a Realtor for Moosehead Realty.

"I told her that I doubted you were interested, but that I'd pass on the message. You aren't, are you? Interested?"

"I don't know." Holly paused to think about it. "Maybe. I mean, what am I going to do with a house that has seven bedrooms and thirty acres to tend to?"

"I don't know. Raise a family," Noel suggested. "I know you keep pointing out that you live in New York now, but we both know that your life is here. I always thought you'd come back someday."

Holly knew that at some point she was going to have to figure out what to do with the monstrosity of a house Meg had left her, but not now. Now she needed to get some sleep. "I don't know what I want to do. I do know that I'm not going to make a decision right now. Go ahead and give Madison my number. I guess I'd be interested in hearing what she has to say, but I promise I won't sell the house before I talk it over with you first. I know Meg left it to me, but in a lot of ways I've always felt like it was *our* home."

"Okay." Noel sounded pacified.

"I love you."

"I love you, too. Call me next week. We still need to talk about Christmas."

"Okay. I will. 'Bye."

Holly hung up the phone and turned off the light. It had been quite a week, and she didn't know if she had the mental energy to make a decision about the house. On the other hand, if Madison had a buyer, it made sense to hear what she had to say. Holly knew Noel hoped she'd move back to Moosehead now that she had the house, but truth be told, even if she decided to move back to her hometown, she had no idea what she'd do with a house as large as the one Meg had left her. Unlike Noel, she had no desire to orchestrate her life around dirty diapers, ballet recitals, and Saturday-morning soccer games.

Chapter 4

Friday, November 29

Meadowview Nursing Home was situated on a large piece of land overlooking the countryside just outside of Fargo. The buildings were all painted an attractive white with green trim, and the grounds were nicely manicured. Ben and Holly arrived at precisely eleven o'clock and were ushered into a large sitting room to wait while the receptionist located John Remington's attendant.

"Mr. Holiday, Ms. Thompson," the young man introduced himself. "My name is Bill Washington."

"Nice to meet you." Ben shook the man's hand.

"I've reserved an office down the hall for your interview. Perhaps we should talk first. Please follow me." The man walked down a freshly waxed hall. Holly noticed that the doors to most of the rooms were open. A few residents were visiting with friends and family members, but most sat alone, staring blankly at television screens.

"Have a seat." He indicated two chairs on the opposite side of the table from where he sat. "The director filled me in briefly on the purpose of your visit with John. I'm sorry to inform you that he's having a particularly bad day today. He spent yesterday with his family for Thanksgiving. He seemed in good spirits when he left here yesterday morning, but he was upset when his son brought him back last evening. He seems more confused than ever today. I'm afraid that the memory loss from his illness comes and goes. Most of the time he lives in a fog in which he can't remember things and is easily confused, but every once in a while, he'll demonstrate perfect clarity. Unfortunately, those times when he seems fine seem to come farther and farther apart."

"I see." Ben seemed to be considering the information the attendant had just provided. "We'd like to speak to him anyway, if that's okay. That is, if you think our interview won't do him any harm."

"I don't see why talking to him would confuse him any more than he already is, but I wouldn't expect much. Stay here and I'll get him."

"How awful to lose your memory that way," Holly whispered. "I hope our questions don't upset him."

"If they do, we'll stop," Ben promised. "My great-grandpa Holiday suffered from Alzheimer's before he died. Sometimes his memory loss really bothered him, but at other times he didn't seem to realize there were things he should remember but didn't."

The attendant ushered John into the room several minutes later. "John, I'd like you to meet Ben and Holly."

The older man stopped near the door and frowned. He looked at them as if trying to make them fit into his limited memory.

"Stella?" John walked over and touched Holly's hand.

"No, my name is Holly." Holly smiled at the man, trying to put him at ease.

"Where's Stella?" John looked around the room.

"Stella's not here." The attendant showed John to his chair. "This is Ben and Holly. They'd like to ask you some questions about an incident that happened quite a while ago. Is that okay?"

"Is Stella coming?"

"No, John. Stella's at home. You just saw her yesterday. Stella is John's daughter," the attendant explained.

"John," Ben started, "we'd like to ask you about something that happened a long time ago. Twenty-seven years, to be exact. There was an accident. A young couple died, but you managed to save the baby that was in the backseat. Do you remember that?"

"Stella's baby was in an accident?" John appeared to be upset. "But I just saw her."

"No, Stella's baby wasn't in an accident. This was a different baby, a long time ago. The baby you saved was Holly."

John looked at Holly. She smiled.

"I want to thank you for saving me." Holly placed her hand over his. "If you hadn't come along, I would have died in that accident. You're a real hero. You saved my life."

John just stared at her blankly, as if trying to process what she was telling him. "Do you have a baby? My Stella has a baby. She has my eyes."

Ben looked at Holly, who shrugged. Obviously, they weren't going to get anything out of John today. Holly couldn't believe how disappointed she was, but it wasn't going to do any good to push. They'd have to try something else.

"Here's my card." Ben opened his wallet to pull out a business card. A piece of paper fell on the table. "If you're able to find out anything at all, please let us know." He handed the card to the attendant. "We'll be on the road for the next several weeks at least, so just call my cell."

John picked up the paper that had fallen out of Ben's wallet and sat staring at it. He frowned, and then stared at Ben, who was still talking to the attendant. "Funny you staying at the same hotel as that couple with the baby."

"You remember them?" Holly sat forward.

"I tried to save them, but it was too late." John shook his head. "The baby was alive, though. Cute little thing. All banged up."

"How do you know the couple with the baby stayed at the same hotel we did?" Ben asked.

"Receipt was on the seat. There was so much blood."

"Did you see anything else? Any other papers or receipts?" Ben tried to keep his voice calm and level so as not to alarm the man.

"No. I had to hurry. I had to get the baby out."

"There were two infant seats and two diaper bags," Holly reminded him. "Did you see any indication that there might have been another baby in the car?"

"The baby was so little. She should have been home with her mom."

Holly and Ben looked at each other.

"You didn't think the baby was with her parents?" Ben asked.

"No. I'm getting tired now. Can I go back to my room?" John looked toward Bill.

"Sure. No problem. We have pudding today."

"Chocolate?"

"I think so. Let's go find out."

Bill stood up. "Wait here. I'll get John settled and come back."

"It sounds like the couple in the car wasn't my parents," Holly whispered. "I wonder who they were, and why I was with them."

"I don't know. Maybe someone from the motel remembers something. I think we should go back there after we finish up here."

"I don't know, Ben. The kid at the desk looked like he wasn't any older than twenty."

"Yeah, but he might know if there's anyone around who worked at the hotel back then. It's the best lead we have at the moment."

"True."

"Sorry to keep you waiting," Bill said as he walked back into the office. "It's best not to let John get too agitated. If he remembers anything else, I'll give you a call. Sometimes when his memory is jogged, he'll remember random things for days. I really hope you find your answers. It must be awful not to know if you have family in this world."

"Thank you." Holly smiled at him. "Please do call if you find out anything at all. You never know what odd piece of information might help."

Ben and Holly left the nursing home and headed back to the motel they had checked out of a few hours earlier.

"You're back. Did you forget something?" the young desk clerk asked when they walked into the lobby.

"Actually, we wanted to ask you a few questions. We're investigating into an accident that happened twenty-seven years ago and have reason to believe whoever worked here at the time might be able to help us. Do you happen to know of anyone who's been around that long?" Ben asked.

"I haven't even been *alive* twenty-seven years, but the motel manager, Mike Bell, might be able to help. He's been here forever. Hang on. I'll get his phone number."

Ben called Mike and spoke with him while Holly went to the restroom. It had been quite a couple of days. She leaned over the sink and splashed water on her face, then let it drip back into the sink. If the couple in the car wasn't her parents, why would she have been with them? And no matter who they were, if the storm that night was so bad, why were they out in it with a brand-new baby? The whole thing was giving her a headache. She dug a couple of aspirin out of her purse and swallowed them.

By the time she returned to the lobby, Ben was off the phone and waiting by the car.

"Did you find out anything?"

"Yes and no. The motel manager did remember the couple and the baby. The baby was white and the couple were Hispanic. He thought it was odd that such a little baby would be traveling with people who weren't her parents. He said the woman seemed awkward with the baby. It was almost as if she had never held a baby before. He also verified that there was just one baby with the couple. He said the couple checked in early in the morning and checked out later that evening. The whole thing struck him as odd; not only was it dark when they decided to leave, but it was 'snowing like the devil,' his words."

"So now what?"

"I guess we head to Gardiner. We should be there by tomorrow afternoon."

"Did you remember to call Noel?" Ben asked once they'd gotten on the road. The storm had cleared, leaving the landscape blanketed in a frosty wonderland that reminded Holly of miles upon miles of freshly whipped cream. By the time they'd left Fargo behind, the sun had already peaked and was beginning its descent due to the short fall days.

"I did. Thanks for reminding me." Holly offered Ben a piece of gum from the pack she'd bought at the gas station where they'd filled the Range Rover's tank. "Noel tends to worry if we don't talk every couple of days. She's a real mother hen. I'm sure deep down she thinks I'd never be able to manage my own life without her guidance and advice."

"Does that bother you?" Ben pulled a piece of gum from the pack and began unwrapping it.

"Not really." Holly folded a piece of gum into her mouth and returned the pack to her purse. "It's nice to know you have someone in the world who cares about you that much. Now that Meg's gone, she's all I have."

"Tommy and Noel must have gotten married young. I seem to remember they have a son who's around ten."

"Tommy and Noel have been together since they were in the eighth grade," Holly confirmed. "There was never anyone else for either of them. They married right out of high school, and Brian was born nine months later. Cassidy was born two years after that, followed by Cody, and then Heather. When I asked her if she was going to stop after Heather, she said one more and she'd have a coed basketball team.

Personally, I think she's nuts, but the kids are really great, and they seem happy."

"Are you planning on having a basketball team of your own someday?" Ben asked.

"Me?" Holly snorted. "No way. I'm not sure I'm the mom type. How about you? Any mini sports teams in your future?"

"Definitely. At least I hope so. I'd like to have a houseful of kids. I grew up with four sisters. I can't imagine not recreating that love and chaos for myself someday."

"Don't take this the wrong way," Holly prefaced, "but it seems to me if you want a houseful of kids, you'd better get started finding a wife. Takes a while to build a family."

"I was engaged once," Ben informed her. "She was a fellow officer. She didn't want quite as many kids as I do, but she was willing to have a couple. I really thought I'd be a dad by now." Ben sounded sad.

"What happened?" Holly knew it wasn't any of her business, but she couldn't seem to stop herself from asking.

"She couldn't understand why I'd be willing to give up my career for my mom. Basically, she offered me an ultimatum: stay on the force and get married as planned or quit and break up for good. In the end, I decided I didn't want to be married to someone who'd engage in emotional blackmail. I quit the force; she gave me back my ring and married an old friend of mine six months later. Last I heard, they're very happy."

"Wow. I'm sorry."

"That's okay." Ben shrugged. "I'm not sure we were ever really right for each other. I think our romance was just based on our mutual decision that it was time to get married and start a family. We had been dating for a while and shared common interests; it made sense that we'd take the next step. In the long run, I'm not sure we would have been happy."

"Maybe you're right. Still, if you want a big family, you must feel your biological clock ticking, or at least the guy equivalent of a biological clock."

"Yeah, sometimes. Too bad you don't want any kids. We seem to make a pretty good team."

Chapter 5

Saturday, November 30

Ben and Holly pulled into the pretty little town of Gardiner at noon on the Saturday after Thanksgiving. The storm they'd encountered in the north must not have worked its way this far south; the streets and sidewalks were free of snow. The town was bustling with holiday shoppers roaming through gift shops looking for a bargain. Normally, Holly ordered her Christmas gifts through mail-order catalogues or online, but the festive music coming from the beautifully decorated shops put her in the holiday spirit. Maybe if she had time, she'd look for something for Jessica and Noel and her family.

"Where do we start?" Holly asked.

"How about lunch?" Ben suggested.

"I could eat."

"After that, I guess we'll start asking around and see where it leads."

They found a cute café that was already decorated for Christmas. After being shown to a table and given menus and cups of coffee, they ordered the house special, then sat back to wait for their meals. *Frosty the Snowman* was playing on the sound system, and for the first time in as long as she could remember, Holly found that she was actually enjoying the jaunty tune about the magical hat that gave life to a pile of snow.

"The waitress looks too young to ask about Carl Langley," Holly commented as she looked around the restaurant for possible informants. "The cook might be old enough, but I doubt it. The woman working the cash register definitely looks old enough, if she lived here back then. Maybe we should start with her."

"Okay. I'll go ask her," Ben volunteered. "If our waitress comes by, ask her for a refill on the coffee."

Holly could see Ben talking to the cashier. He laughed at something she said as she leaned in closer, as if sharing a private joke. *What a flirt.* The woman had to be forty years older than Ben, but Holly could swear she saw her blush at something Ben whispered in her ear. Not that Holly blamed the woman: Ben had been put together about as perfectly as anyone could be assembled. He looked especially gorgeous today in a royal blue sweater and faded jeans, and the sturdy hiking boots he wore gave him a sexy yet manly appeal.

Ben handed the woman one of his business cards and sat down a few minutes later. "She wasn't living here that long ago, but she said we should talk to Wilma Trundle. She's lived here her whole life and knows everything about everyone."

"And where can we find this Wilma Trundle?"

"She said to try the bookstore on the corner. She doesn't usually work weekends, but with the holiday crowd she thought she might be there."

Less than an hour later, Ben and Holly walked down the festively decorated street toward the equally decorated bookstore. A bell jingled as they walked into the quaint shop that sold not only new and used books but local crafts and trinkets. The store looked exactly like the type of place to find something Noel might like. If she had time, perhaps she'd come back later.

"Can I help you?" the elderly woman behind the counter asked.

"We're looking for Wilma Trundle," Ben said.

"Well, you found her. What can I do for you?"

"We were wondering if you remember a man who lived here a long time ago. His name was Carl Langley."

"Sure, I remember Carl." The woman with short white hair and a snowman on her sweater smiled. "An ornerier cuss was never born. He died over twenty-five years ago, God rest his soul. What do you want to know about him?"

"We're investigating my friend Holly's past. She was found in a wrecked vehicle twenty-seven years ago, when she was only days old. The vehicle was registered to Mr. Langley but was driven by a Hispanic couple. We were hoping that someone in the area might have some information that could help us."

The woman stopped to consider what Ben had said. "Carl kept to himself. Never even came into town except now and then for supplies. He did have a Hispanic couple who worked for him from time to time, but I can't say that I remember their names. You might try talking to Lilly Walton. She owns the ranch that borders the one Carl owned. She used to drop in now and then to check on him. She's the one who found him dead."

"Can you tell us how we can reach her?" Holly asked

"I can give you her number, but she's up north visiting her daughter for the holiday. She told me she wouldn't be back until late Monday night. She doesn't carry a cell phone, but you should be able to reach her at home on Tuesday morning."

"Thanks for your help." Ben took the hastily scribbled phone number from the woman. "Here's my card. If you think of anything else, please give us a call."

"Now what?" Holly asked as they left the store and crossed the street toward the parking lot where they'd left the Range Rover.

"Have you ever driven through Yellowstone and Grand Teton National Parks?"

"No, I can't say that I have."

"We're sitting at the gateway. I say we take advantage of that. We can stay here tonight, drive through the parks to Jackson, Wyoming, tomorrow, spend the night there, and drive back Monday. We'll give Ms. Walton a call on Tuesday."

"Are you sure? I feel like we're wasting two days. Maybe we should regroup and see if we can pick up another lead."

"We really don't have any other leads at this point," Ben pointed out. "Let's have some fun and then see what happens when Lilly Walton gets back."

"Oh, yeah." Holly sighed. "I'm supposed to be *that* Holly. Fun Holly." She shrugged. "Okay, I'm in."

The small town was booked up for the holiday weekend, but Ben happened to find rooms in a small bed-and-breakfast for the night. After checking in, they dropped off their suitcases and headed back toward the downtown area to do a little holiday shopping.

"Long list?" Holly asked Ben.

"Not too bad. I usually get something for my mom and Marty, my three sisters, their husbands, and my six nieces. How about you?"

"Noel and her family and my assistant Jessica and boss Phillip. I have a neighbor who waters my plants when I'm gone, so I usually get her something. Other than the normal tokens for people like my hairdresser and the pizza delivery guy, that's pretty much it."

"You buy a gift for the pizza delivery guy?" Ben asked.

"I order a lot of pizza. Not really one to cook."

"Okay." Ben paused at a quaint gift shop featuring locally crafted gifts. "Where do we start?"

"Well," Holly hesitated, "I saw a pair of earrings in a window earlier that I think I'd like to have for myself. How about we start there? After that we can look for a toy store for the kids, although we might want to wait until we get back to New York for that."

"Are you going to Moosehead for Christmas this year?" Ben asked as they walked toward the shop with the earrings.

"I don't know. Probably not, although Noel has been campaigning for me to come home for over a month, and experience has shown that she tends to wear me down after a bit. If I do give in and go, I'll probably only stay a few days."

"Missing Meg?"

"Yeah. It'll be so strange to be in Moosehead and not have her there. I planned to stay in New York this year and work, but now? I don't know. I guess I'll just see where I'm at when the time comes. Oh, look." Holly grabbed Ben's arm and pointed toward a side street that opened onto a large meadow. "A sleigh ride. Want to try it?"

"I'm game." Ben shrugged.

Ben paid the man, then helped Holly onto the backseat of the large, ten-seat sleigh. The first six seats were filled, but seats seven through nine remained empty, giving the back of the sleigh an intimate feel. Ben wrapped a blanket he found on the seat around the two of them as the sleigh set off toward Yellowstone National Park.

Families with young children occupied the front of the sleigh, so the driver led the group through familiar Christmas carols as four beautiful Clydesdales pulled them along a groomed trail that looked as though it hadn't received fresh snow for quite some time.

Holly rested her head on Ben's shoulder as he held her hand under the blanket. They sat together in silence as the beauty of the area unfolded around them. The open meadow gave way to a cozy trail bordered on both sides by towering pines that almost blocked out the light from the moon. Snow began to fall gently as she closed her eyes and let the magic of the bells attached to the harness meld with the sound of children's voices raised in song. Ben's body felt warm next to her, causing her to feel happy and content, emotions she hadn't experienced for quite some time.

"Meg has a sleigh," Holly said, breaking the silence. "Or at least she had one. I'm not sure what happened to it."

"Huh," Ben responded vaguely, as if he was unsure where Holly intended to steer the conversation.

"When I was a kid, if we had enough snow, we'd all pile into the sleigh on Christmas Eve and ride into town. Meg would drive that old sleigh up and down Main Street while all the kids who were living with us sang carols and drank hot chocolate. After that we'd all go to Christmas services."

"Sounds like fun." Ben cuddled in closer.

"It was. At first. I still remember the year I turned thirteen, though," Holly continued. "I was convinced that I was too old for such foolishness and absolutely refused to go along with the younger kids. I knew Meg was hurt by my refusal to participate in what had become something of a tradition for us, but my fear that my middle-school peers would see me and think it was dumb won out, and I stayed home in spite of Meg's feelings. She tried to act like she wasn't upset so as not to ruin the trip for the younger kids, but I knew how hurt she was. That was the last year she made the trip. The next December she made up some excuse about the sleigh needing new runners, but I knew by the look in her eye that I'd ruined it for her."

"Sounds like you still feel bad about it."

"I do," Holly agreed. "But what I really feel bad about is the fact that I didn't feel worse about it at the time. I knew I'd hurt Meg, but part of me didn't care."

"Sounds like a typical teenager," Ben commented as he gently wiped away the snow that had fallen on Holly's hair.

"Yeah, I guess, but I sure wish I had it to do over again."

"Part of being a parent is understanding that sometimes kids do hurtful things," Ben pointed out. "I think that in the end Meg remembered the good times and not the bad. Do you know her favorite when-Holly-was-a-kid story?"

Holly cringed, as Ben turned slightly to look toward the front of the sleigh, which was gliding past an entire herd of elk. "Do I want to know?"

"When you were four or maybe five," he began, "she'd just taken in a new charge, a teenager who had just been bounced from her fifth foster home."

"Tiffany," Holly supplied.

"Sounds right. I guess Tiffany was a real handful, with a lot of pent-up rage, and she pretty much alienated the other kids on the first day she was there. Anyway, Meg said that every day for a week she'd go in to clean Tiffany's room and find a Baggie with staples hidden somewhere in the room. Initially, she thought Tiffany was saving up staples in order to do something dangerous with them. She confronted her, but the girl swore she didn't have any idea where they had come from. Meg decided to move the box of staples from the den into her room, which she said was off limits to the kids, but still, every day, staples."

Holly smiled as he spoke. She knew exactly where the story was going but let him continue. Somehow the smooth harmony of his baritone voice made the story seem much more interesting than it really was.

"Anyway, as I guess you already know, Meg eventually found out that you were the one who was stealing the staples and hiding them in various places in Tiffany's room."

"I'd overheard Meg telling the social worker that Tiffany's real problem was that she was missing stables in her life. Meg meant things like a stable environment and stable discipline, but I thought she said staples, so I started stealing them from Meg and giving them to Tiffany," Holly finished.

"Meg must have told that story at least ten times during the two years I knew her. She was proud that you were softhearted enough to want to help the girl who was behaving so abrasively that the other kids avoided her."

"She actually ended up staying with Meg until she turned eighteen," Holly informed him. "She was at the funeral. Tall woman with long black hair who sat in the front row next to Noel."

"Yeah, I saw her," Ben confirmed. "Beautiful woman."

Holly couldn't believe she was actually jealous of that innocent statement. "Looks like we're heading back. This has been fun. Sorry I got all serious on you. I seem to be doing that a lot lately. The guy I was seeing a few months ago broke up with me because he said that every conversation we had, no matter where we started, looped back around to Meg."

"The fact that every conversation gets back to Meg is completely understandable." Ben hugged her closer to his side. "She was the single most important person in your life and now she's gone. Don't beat yourself up over the fact that you miss her."

Holly smiled.

"While this ride has been both beautiful and informative," Ben added, "I'm freezing my keister off. How about we find a cozy little bar and have a hot toddy? I think I saw a place with a big fireplace when we were in town earlier."

"Sounds perfect."

Chapter 6

Sunday, December 1

The scenery through Yellowstone was some of the most beautiful Holly had ever seen. The area had received a light dusting of snow the night before, and evergreen branches hung low from their towering heights as icicles weighed down the dark green needles of the majestic trees. Colorful hot springs bubbled up through the frozen terrain, painting the countryside in reds, yellows, blues, and oranges. And most spectacular of all were the fountains of hot water that shot out of the ground as the parks many geysers erupted with timeless precision.

Giant elk and once endangered buffalo wearing thick winter coats grazed on the golden tundra peeking up through the snow-covered ground. Ben wrapped his arms around a shivering Holly as they waited in the frigid air with hundreds of other visitors for Old Faithful to display her geothermal majesty.

"It seems that Old Faithful isn't being all that faithful today." Holly snuggled into Ben's arms as she leaned into his powerful chest.

He rested his chin on the top of Holly's head. "Contrary to popular belief, Old Faithful doesn't go off every hour on the hour as some people think, but trust me, it's worth the wait. Once she does blow, she'll shoot well over a hundred feet straight up into the air, erupting in a display that's not only awesome in terms of raw power but demonstrates grace, beauty, and symmetry as well. The first time I saw it, I was blown away by its impact. To think that it's probably been here for thousands of years, erupting every seventy minutes or so whether or not anyone is here to see it. With so many spectators, it's hard to remember that it's not just some water show like they have at those fancy Las Vegas casinos, but something so much more."

Holly turned to stare at this amazing man, who felt so deeply about something as otherwise unemotional as a geothermal event. She was glad she'd come to Yellowstone for the first time with Ben. If she'd have come on her own, she probably would have snapped a few pictures and been on her way without stopping to consider the grandeur of such a special place. "It looks like she's starting to do something." Holly stood on tiptoe and tried to see over the heads of the crowd around her. Several short spurts of water shot into the air, each one shooting a little higher than the one before.

"Climb up onto that tree stump," Ben instructed. "You'll get a better view. I'll hang on to you so you won't fall."

Holly carefully climbed up onto the stump, which stood a good four feet tall. Ben steadied her as she balanced her weight on the uneven surface. He wrapped his arm around her hips as she held on to his shoulder for support.

"Oh, wow, look at that." She stared over the heads in front of her in wonder at the majesty she was witnessing. "It's so . . . wow."

All at once, without warning, the geyser sent thousands of gallons of water spewing into the heavens. Holly jerked backward in response to the powerful spray and fell safely into Ben's arms.

"Good catch." She laughed as she wrapped her arms around his neck.

"Worked out better than I expected." Ben leaned forward very slowly and kissed the woman he still held. He gently caressed her lips with his own as the geyser continued to erupt, sending a series of oohs and ahhs through the crowd surrounding them.

The cheering crowd faded into the background as Holly focused all her attention on Ben's gentle but oh so tantalizing lips. She had been kissed many times by many different people, but never before had a kiss felt so intensely spiritual. As Ben's lips moved slowly and reverently over hers, she could feel their souls connect in a brief instant of karmic harmony.

By the time Ben ended the kiss, Old Faithful had peaked, and with her final eruption, the crowd around them had begun to disperse. Ben took several deep breaths before releasing Holly's legs and letting her body slide slowly down his until her feet reached the ground.

"Wow, that was really something," Holly choked.

"There's a coffee shop inside the visitor center." Ben took a step back. "How about we get some lunch before we continue south?"

"Sounds good." Holly tried to take a step forward and stumbled. Ben put his arm around her to steady her. She leaned into his side, letting him lead her across the parking lot and into the warmth of the Yellowstone Visitor Center.

Holly picked at her hamburger as she tried to figure Ben out. One minute he was kissing her with a passion she had never before experienced, and the next he was eating a roast beef sandwich and chattering on about the area's unique geothermal activity. Couldn't he hear her heart pounding even now? Was he still hung up on his ex-fiancée or was he simply not all that attracted to her? It had been a while since she'd dipped her toe into the dating pool. Maybe somewhere along the way she'd lost all ability to tell when a man was interested in her and when he was just passing time. Jessica was certain that Derek thought they were dating, while that idea had never entered her mind. Maybe she was as clueless about reading the signals the men in her life were giving off as everyone around her seemed to think.

"It's really the relationship between the earth and the water that falls from above that causes such a phenomenon," Ben explained. "When the upthrust of the Rocky Mountains . . ."

"Upthrust?" Holly interrupted.

"Have you even heard one thing I've said?"

"Sure. Every word. Actually, not really. Sorry. I guess I'm just distracted."

"Do you want to talk about it?"

"Not really. It's just that . . ." Holly looked up at Ben's lips as he licked mustard from his finger. "I was just thinking about what news Lilly might have for us," she lied.

"This has been hard on you, digging into a past you didn't even know you had until a few days ago."

"Yeah, I guess. But I'm having fun, too. Yellowstone is more beautiful than anything I'd ever imagined. And Old Faithful"—Holly felt her palms begin to sweat in spite of the nippy temperature— "let's just say I can't even begin to describe how that made me feel."

Ben cleared his throat and took a huge gulp of his ice water. "Yeah, it was really something."

"I can't wait to see what comes next." Holly hoped that Ben understood that she wasn't talking about the scenery. She hoped that the come-hither look she was trying for accurately conveyed her interest in getting to know the man on a more romantic level. She didn't think she wanted to complicate her life with messy entanglements, but there was something about Ben that she instinctively knew would make messy worth her while.

"Let's finish up and we'll be on our way." Ben pushed away his unfinished sandwich and picked up the check the waitress had already left on the table. "There's a short hike in the Tetons that will take your breath away. If we don't get a move on, we won't have time to take it and still arrive in Jackson before dark."

The harsh majesty of the Teton Mountains was as breathtaking as the spectacular geysers of Yellowstone. Bold, jagged spires of rock reached high into the sky as low-lying clouds masked the highest peaks, giving the illusion that the towering mountain reached up to heaven itself. Ben pulled into a deserted parking area at the foot of the mountain, where a narrow dirt path disappeared into a grove of aspen trees.

"I thought Yellowstone was breathtaking, but this is truly amazing." Holly gazed in wonder at the rugged peaks in the distance. "I feel like I'm looking at something magical. Like Alice's rabbit hole."

"Alice's rabbit hole?"

"Alice went through a magical rabbit hole and found Wonderland. It feels like you could climb to the top of that mountain and walk into the gates of heaven and discover all the secrets contained within."

"It is beautiful, isn't it? Come on. I want to show you something." Ben opened the car door and stepped out onto the dirt lot. He walked her down the path and through the grove of now-dormant trees toward a beautiful mountain lake at the base of a rocky cliff.

"Wow. It's gorgeous," Holly breathed.

"As spectacular as the winter landscape is, you should come back earlier in the fall. The bright golden leaves of the aspen trees in the area provide a spectacular contrast to the ruggedness of the mountain. Maybe we'll come back next October. It's mating season for the elk, another wondrous site to behold."

"It's a date." Holly closed her eyes, holding Ben's words close to her heart. Part of her prayed that Ben would still be a part of her life when the trees turned colors next year, but part of her also realized that scenario was highly unlikely, given the fact that there was nowhere for their relationship to go. He lived in Moosehead; she lived in New York. He wanted a house full of kids and she'd pretty much decided that motherhood wasn't for her.

"The hike I was talking about leads up the mountain. We don't have time to go to the end, but there are some spectacular views near the bottom if you're up for it," Ben suggested.

"Sounds like you've been here before."

"I have, several times."

The pair started down the trail side by side. "We drove through when I was really young. I don't remember much from that trip, but I came with my dad a few years later. My sisters all wanted to go somewhere tropical for our annual vacation, but my dad and I wanted to go fishing, so my mom took the girls to Hawaii and Dad and I came here for two weeks. Just the two of us. In some ways, it was the best two weeks of my life. I was only six at the time and don't remember everything about the trip, but I do remember the campfires my dad built every night. We'd sit around and talk about guy stuff. I felt like a man for the first time in my life. I think that trip was a real turning point for us. Prior to that, my mom considered me too young to go off alone with my dad, who was a fantastic parent but not quite as protective as my mom would have liked."

"What do you mean?"

"My mom is a wonderful person, but she has a tendency to overparent, if you know what I mean. When I was growing up, she was all about being safe and following the rules and being responsible. My dad, in contrast, was more about letting us do what we wanted to do so long as we were responsible for the consequences of our actions. I think my mom was afraid my dad was going to let me do something dangerous if she wasn't there to keep an eye on things."

"And did he," Holly wondered, "let you do something dangerous?"

"Actually, yeah." Ben chuckled. "I came home from that trip with both a new understanding of what it meant to be a man and my very first broken arm."

Holly's eyes opened wide in surprise.

"A rope swing swung out over the lake," Ben explained. "I miscalculated when to let go and ended up on the beach instead of in the water."

"Oh no. Did your mom ever let you go off with your dad again?"

"Yeah, once she got over being mad. How about you? Any broken arms in your past?"

"Three," Holly informed him.

"Seriously?"

"What can I say?" Holly shrugged. "I was a tomboy who made it my goal in life to keep up with my older foster brothers. Meg had taken in twin brothers. They were only a year older than me, but they were already on their third foster home, so they had this mature detachment I found fascinating. One really hot summer day, when Meg was busy with laundry, the boys convinced Noel and me to sneak out of the house to go swimming in the frog pond. There was this big rock that the kids in town dove off of into the water. Meg used to take us swimming in the pond, but she never let us climb the rock and dive off. So, of course, the first thing we did was climb the rock. The others all came away unscathed, but I ended up with my first broken arm."

"And the second one?" Ben asked as the trail wound steeply up the side of the mountain. The trail was free of ice, but the narrow walkway, coupled with a steep drop-off, made the trip perilous none the same.

"Kenny Baker and I tried to fly by attaching paper wings to our arms and jumping off the roof of the barn. Wow, look at the view!" Holly gasped as they came around a corner to find a spectacular vista of the entire valley.

"It's beautiful, isn't it?"

"Breathtaking."

Ben put his arm around Holly's shoulders as they enjoyed the absolute perfection of the moment. Thousands of elk had congregated in a large meadow at the edge of the valley. A hunter's paradise, if not for the strict regulations protecting them. Holly put her head on Ben's shoulder as they enjoyed the moment in perfect silence.

The air was crisp, but the sun was shining, bringing a feeling of warmth to their face and shoulders. Holly took a deep breath as she took in the scent of Ben's cologne. She knew that this exact moment in time would be forever etched in her memory, in spite of whatever else might occur in the weeks ahead.

"And did you?" Ben's deep voice pierced the silence.

"Did I what?"

"Fly?"

Holly smiled. "Yeah, for a brief second. It was such an awesome feeling that when Xander Collins suggested building an airplane and pushing if off of the bluff when I was eleven, I was all for it."

"Broken arm number three?" Ben guessed.

"It was worth it. That little plane actually glided for quite a ways before it hit a tree and came crashing down. We were able to build wings to carry it, but we never did figure out how to steer it."

"I'm surprised that an eleven-year-old could manage to build something that could fly."

"Xander was a smart kid who grew up to be an even smarter adult. He builds real planes for the military. Secret spy stuff."

"Sounds like you had an adventurous childhood."

"It was the best." It had been a long time since Holly had looked back at who she was before she moved to New York and became Dear Holly, a sophisticated advice columnist who wore designer suits and went to five-hundred-dollar-a-plate fund-raisers and often spent more on a pair of shoes than she did on her rent.

Jackson, Wyoming, was a small town nestled at the foot of the Teton Mountains. Its world-class status was evidenced by its upscale restaurants, luxury hotels, and name-brand boutiques. The narrow streets were crowded with holiday shoppers and hungry skiers who were just coming down off the mountain after a day on the slopes.

"I hope we don't have any trouble finding a hotel with vacancies," Ben commented as he tried to navigate traffic.

"There's one up on the left that looks nice. Pull over and I'll see if they have any rooms," Holly volunteered.

She jogged into the lobby while Ben waited in the double-parked car. After several minutes she came out and slid back into the passenger seat.

"The desk clerk said the entire town is sold out, but he had one last-minute cancellation he could give us. It's four hundred dollars a night, and he only has the one room, but it has two beds."

"Is one room okay with you?"

Holly shrugged, trying to sell a level of indifference she was far from feeling. "Sure, why not?"

"Okay, run back in and tell him we'll take it. I'll find a parking spot and come in to pay for it."

After checking into their single room with two queen-size beds, Ben and Holly decided to take a walk and see the town, which had been transformed into a Christmas village, complete with white twinkling lights, green garlands, and red bows hanging from every lamppost. The eclectic shops on the main street were cheerfully decorated, and jaunty Christmas carols played in almost every store. Throngs of shoppers wandered from one store to another along the wooden boardwalks, in search of the perfect gift or vacation souvenir.

"It feels like we're in Santa's Village," Holly commented.

"I was just thinking the same thing," Ben said. "Every single shop is decorated and playing music."

"I especially love the window displays." Holly stopped in front of the large bay window of a furniture store that had a miniature town, complete with a working ski lift and a miniature train. "Check out the ice skaters." She pointed to a replica of a pond in the middle of a dense forest. Several bystanders sat on park benches as skaters of all ages moved to the music. In the forest beyond the miniature pond, deer, bears, and cottontail bunnies watched with interest.

"It's been years since I've been skating," Ben admitted.

"I'd be willing to bet they have a real skating rink somewhere in the area, if you're interested," Holly said.

"As fun as that sounds, it's getting late and I'm starving. How about we look for a place to get something to eat instead?"

They walked hand in hand along the wooden walkway, looking in windows and telling each other stories of Christmases past. Holly told Ben the story of her first bike and Ben told her about his first real bow and arrow. Both shared remembrances of decorating trees, family dinners, and school plays. While Ben had grown up in a large family with biological siblings and Holly had spent her youth in a large family of temporary ones, both agreed that there was nothing that spelled Christmas like a large house filled with people you loved.

"Oh, wow." Holly stuck her head into an old-fashioned saloon with a huge wooden bar, hardwood floors scattered with peanut shells, and walls adorned with rusty antiques. "I love this place. Let's have a drink."

They found seats on tall wooden bar stools and ordered shots of whiskey, in keeping with the Old West theme. Bowls of peanuts still in the shell were passed out as boisterous patrons sipped frosty mugs of beer and shared stories of their day on the slopes.

"Isn't this great?" Holly looked around at the antiques displayed throughout the bar. "It feels festive and joyful and energetic. Can you imagine this place a hundred years ago, when it was filled with cowboys and miners and not preppy skiers? When I come to an old building like this, I feel like I'm living a piece of history. I can close my eyes and imagine the patrons of times past. It's so romantic. Don't you think it's romantic?"

"Kind of reminds me of that old hunting lodge up near the Canadian border."

"Grizzly's," Holly guessed. "I love that place. Personally, I could do without the animal heads on the walls, but the food is fantastic and the view is spectacular."

"Next time you're in Moosehead, we'll go," Ben promised. "I haven't been that far north for years. Been meaning to make the trip."

"Aunt Meg used to take us every year for Lumberjack Days. It's been a few years since I've been, but as long as you have plenty of sunscreen and mosquito repellent, a good time can be had. Some of the guys who compete are really talented. I especially like the log-rolling competition."

"Another drink?" the waitress asked.

"We should probably start thinking about where we want to have dinner," Ben suggested. "Whiskey on an empty stomach isn't usually a good idea. I saw a nice little Italian place a few doors down. Do you like Italian?"

"Love it."

"Italian it is then." Ben paid the bill and they walked down the street to the restaurant. It had started to snow while they were in the bar, and huge fluffy flakes danced their way toward the ground as holiday music penetrated each storefront. The Italian restaurant was situated between an adorable shop selling mountain-themed housewares and a used bookstore that had Holly itching to explore.

In spite of the fact that the town was busy, Ben managed to procure a table with less than a ten-minute wait. He ordered old-fashioned spaghetti and meatballs, and Holly chose lasagna. They started the meal with crisp Italian salads and crusty garlic bread. The bottle of wine they shared was the finest cabernet, and the heat from the fire in the old stone fireplace near their table left Holly feeling relaxed and languid.

"Have you been to Jackson before?" Holly asked.

"A couple of times. The first was with my family, when I was three. My parents thought it was important for us to know this great country we live in, so they rented an RV and we all went on a road trip."

"Across the whole country?" Holly couldn't imagine taking a trip like that with five kids.

"Pretty much. Started out in New York, then sort of zigzagged across the northern half of the country, stopping to catch what my parents considered the highlights. After we reached the West Coast, we turned around and came back across the southern half."

"Wow. That sounds . . ." *awful*, Holly thought, "interesting."

"Honestly, I don't remember much about that trip." Ben smiled. "One day I hope to do it with my own family."

Growing up in a foster home with a foster mother who was always willing to take in one more needy child, in spite of the fact that they were already bursting at the seams, had left Holly with a vast appreciation for quiet and solitude. She liked living alone, and her idea of a vacation was two weeks at a tropical resort, not a month or more driving across the country with five children. She could feel herself being drawn to Ben, with his crooked smile and kind heart, but she knew deep down inside that they were much too different to ever share anything long-term. It was best she remembered that before she fell hopelessly in love.

Chapter 7

Monday, December 2

The next morning, Holly opened her eyes and found Ben staring down at her. She touched a hand to her hair and grimaced. She must look a fright. She placed her hand over her mouth before sitting up and asking what he was looking at. Morning breath wasn't something she wanted to share this early in their relationship, or maybe she should say their nonrelationship.

"I was just watching you sleep. You're really quite adorable. You have a little drool." He pointed to the corner of her mouth.

Oh God.

Holly bolted into the bathroom without saying anything more. She turned the shower on hot and stood under it, wondering if anyone had ever actually died of embarrassment. Closing her eyes, she put her hands against the wall in front of her and let the hot spray pound over her head, neck, and shoulders.

Agreeing to share a room the previous evening had been the worst decision she'd made in a long time. Or maybe it was the best. She'd encouraged Ben to tell her his most closely guarded secrets, freeing up any inhibitions she might have had to respond in kind. She'd laughed at his hilarious tales of his childhood, groaned at the embarrassing moments of his adolescence, and cried at the more touching points in his adult life. He, in turn, laughed, groaned, and cried with her. It had been a long time since she'd shared such a deeply intimate evening with anyone with whom she wasn't actually having a deeply intimate relationship.

Applying shampoo to her wet hair, she reminded herself that becoming emotionally attached to Ben was out of the question. Her life plan, which she'd put a lot of thought into developing, didn't allow for serious dating for another five years. As she rinsed her hair, she realized that, while perfect in every way, Ben had come along much, much too soon. If she was going to have the life she'd dreamed of, she was going to need to take a step back and focus on her outcomes. She'd find her family, syndicate her column, move into the fast lane, and maybe, if Ben was still available in six or eight years . . .

Holly wandered down to the hotel restaurant after drying her hair and dressing in a pair of jeans and a warm blue sweater. The minute she saw Ben sitting at a table for two in a small alcove next to a huge picture window, she knew she was kidding herself if she thought she could put this man on hold. Yes, her career was important to her, and no, she didn't need a man to complete her, but maybe, just maybe, she needed Ben.

Snow was falling in thick sheets beyond the gaily decorated windowpanes, making visibility almost nil. She walked across the room in tune to the holiday music playing softly in the background. "It's really coming down." She sat down across from Ben as a waitress hurried over to fill her white ceramic coffee mug.

"The road through the national parks we took yesterday is closed. We'll have to go the long way around."

"Long way?"

"There's a road that runs north through Idaho that will get us to our destination, but it'll take a little longer. Probably an extra day in this snow."

Holly looked out of the window at the white landscape. Huge flakes covered tire tracks in the road just moments after the vehicles drove by. "It's snowing pretty hard. Do you think we should just wait out the storm and try to go back through the parks tomorrow?"

"Once they close the roads through the parks, they generally stay closed for the entire winter. I'm afraid US 20 is our only choice. I just hope it stays open. Otherwise, we'll have to take Interstate 15 north, which will take us significantly out of our way. I checked with the highway patrol when I came down, and at this point Highway 20 is open for four-wheel drive vehicles and cars with chains."

"I guess it's a good thing you have four-wheel drive. Maybe we should get going right away."

Ben stopped to consider. "I think we should go ahead and eat something before we start out. The road we'll be taking is used mostly by campers and people with summer cabins. There may not be anywhere to stop along the way. I have an emergency kit in the back of the Range Rover with blankets, flashlights, and flares, that sort of thing. I think we should stop off at the mini-mart, though, and stock up on some nonperishable food and bottled water."

"May I take your order?" the pretty brunette waitress said, interrupting them.

"I'll have the manager's omelet with wheat toast," Ben answered.

"I'll have the same." Holly had no idea what the manager's omelet consisted of, but she hadn't had a chance to look at the menu and didn't want to take the time to do so. She looked nervously out of the window at the falling snow. She loved snow, but driving through a blizzard on an isolated road brought back memories she couldn't possibly have.

"We can cut over to Interstate 15 if you'd be more comfortable." Ben placed his hand over Holly's.

"I don't want to waste any more time than we have to. I'm really anxious to talk to Lilly Walton. Maybe if she knows who the couple in the car was, she'll also know why I was with them, and where the second baby was. I'm having a hard time wrapping my head around this whole thing. I'm not even sure what I feel at this point. I just know I need to find out for certain what happened, and whether or not I have a sister out there."

"You realize that Lilly might not be able to tell us any more than we already know?" Ben cautioned Holly. "You know I'll do everything I can to help you find your answers, but we're trying to solve a twenty-seven-year-old mystery that the police and other authorities couldn't solve at the time of the incident. The odds aren't in our favor. I just don't want you to be too disappointed if we hit a dead end."

"I'm afraid it's too late for that. A week ago I didn't even know I might have a sister, and now I feel like she'll haunt me my entire life if we don't find her." Holly looked directly into Ben's eyes. "I have to find her. No matter how long it takes. I need to know what happened."

"Okay then, we'll keep looking until we find your answers. Now eat your breakfast. I'll see if the waitress can make us some coffee for the road. It's going to be a long day."

Seven hours and less than two hundred miles later, they were inching along a particularly bad part of highway. The snow had been coming down steadily all day and the wind had caused drifts to pile up along the road. Holly could feel the tension in her stomach as the storm worsened. The terrain they'd been traveling was desolate and lonely. They hadn't seen another car in hours.

"It doesn't look like a plow's even been through here." Holly squinted as she tried to make out the narrow borders ahead of them.

"Take a look at that map and see if there are any towns up ahead we might be able to stop in for the night."

"I have no idea where we even are."

"We crossed into Montana a while back. We should be just north of the Route 287 intersection."

Holly turned on the overhead light and unfolded the map. "It looks like there's a town called Ennis about forty miles ahead. I have no idea whether they have lodging or not, but it seems our best bet."

"At this pace, it'll take hours to go forty miles and it's getting dark. I'm not sure I'll be able to follow the road once the light fades. See if my cell phone has any reception." Ben pulled the phone out of his pocket and handed it to Holly.

"Sorry, no."

"Okay, we'll continue on as far as we can. If it gets too bad, we'll spend the night in the car and pray for a snowplow before morning."

Ben continued inching the Range Rover forward, using the snow poles along the highway as a rough guide. The drifts completely covered the road's surface in places, making navigating almost impossible.

Holly watched him rub his eyes as he tried to focus against the glare on the icy surface. The snow swirling in front of the headlights had a hypnotic affect on them, leaving them dizzy if they didn't shift their eyes to the side every few minutes.

"I see a light up ahead." Holly's tired voice penetrated the tense darkness. "Off to the left. Maybe it's a house. They might know where we can stay for the night or, at the very least, they might have a phone."

Ben rubbed his eyes again and squinted in the direction Holly was pointing. The light came into view briefly, only to disappear once again as the thick groves of trees and hilly countryside blocked it.

"There's no way I'm going to risk getting off this road unless we come across a driveway or side road. Keep your eyes on the light; hopefully the road curves up ahead and we'll see where to turn."

"It's not a house, it's a car," Holly said almost ten minutes later. "It looks like it slid into a ditch. I hope everyone's okay."

Ben stopped the Range Rover as close to the partially buried vehicle as he dared and opened his door. "Wait here. I'll check it out and be right back."

He went over to the car, stuck his head in through the front window, spoke to someone for several minutes, and came back.

"There's a woman in the car. A very pregnant woman. She's in labor. She was home alone and tried to drive into town to get help and her car slid off the road. Help me fold down the backseats. We'll use the emergency blankets and try to make her as comfortable as possible."

Holly jumped out of the vehicle to help Ben. "You said she's in labor. How much in labor are we talking? Are we going to be able to get her to a hospital in time?"

"I doubt it."

Holly helped Ben fold the blankets to create a makeshift bed in the back of the SUV. It wasn't the Hilton, but under the circumstances it would have to do.

"I was afraid of that. I don't suppose you've ever delivered a baby?"

"It's a piece of cake," Ben assured her. "The main things we have to do at this point are get her warmed up and make her as comfortable as possible. I think we have a little time. We'll get as far as we can. She said this is her first child. They usually take a little longer."

After fashioning the makeshift bed, Ben and Holly trudged through knee-deep snow toward the other vehicle. Ben gently picked up the woman in his arms and walked carefully back to the Range Rover.

"I'm so glad you all came along when you did. I don't know what I'd have done if you hadn't. The car was stuck and I couldn't get it free. I didn't have any service on my cell phone, and there was no way I was going to be able to walk out of here. I haven't seen another vehicle in the two hours or so I've been here. I just prayed for the good lord to send help, and here you are. Bless you."

The woman settled onto the blankets in the back of the Range Rover.

"Do you live in the area?" Holly asked.

"Yeah, about thirty miles down the road. My husband had to go to Billings to tend to his sick mother. He's only going to be gone for a few days. I thought I'd be fine on my own. I'm not due for five weeks, and my friend was supposed to drive in and stay with me. They closed the road from Idaho Falls on account of the snow, though, and she couldn't get through."

The woman gasped and held her stomach. She breathed deeply for several seconds before continuing her story. "I started having contractions a few hours ago and knew I needed to get help."

"The next town is still quite a ways down the road." Ben tucked the heavy blanket around the shivering woman. "Do you happen to know of anywhere closer we could go for help? Maybe a neighbor?"

"There's a camp up ahead. 'Bout ten miles or so. It's a summer camp, but the caretaker is usually there year-round."

"Okay. You just lay back and we'll see if we can get you to the camp. Maybe they have a phone. We can call the hospital and have them send an ambulance. At the very least, maybe they can send a plow." Ben closed the back door and buckled himself into the driver's seat. "By the way, my name is Ben, and this is Holly."

"Mary." The woman gasped and held her side. "The driveway to the camp is about ten miles ahead on the left. Hopefully someone plowed the drive. There will be a sign that says 'camp closed for the season.' Just follow the drive straight back and it'll take you to the caretaker's cottage."

Ben put the vehicle in low-range four-wheel drive and began to make his way slowly down the road. The snow had let up, making visibility a little better, although the night sky had grown completely dark while they'd been stopped on the side of the road. Holly wasn't a particularly religious person, but she found herself praying nonetheless. The poor woman sounded like she was in agony.

"In about three quarters of a mile or so the road will straighten out as it travels through a little valley. Just keep your eyes on the snow poles," the woman directed. "There's about a four-foot shoulder, so just stay about five feet to the left of the poles and you'll be fine. The drive will be about two miles up the road after it starts to wind up the next mountain pass."

"You know this area well. Have you lived here long?" Holly asked, trying to distract both of them from what was really happening.

"About ten years. I drive this road frequently, which is why I thought I could make the trip into town with no problems. I hit an icy patch about the same time as a contraction grabbed hold of my belly and ended up giving the car too much gas. I spun into the ditch before I even knew what happened. If you folks hadn't happened along, I'd have had to deliver my baby all by myself in the backseat of a freezing-cold car. I've birthed calves before, but the idea of trying to deliver my own little boy left me terrified."

"For the first time since we left Jackson this morning, I'm glad we decided on this route. Don't worry. Ben was a cop. He's delivered lots of babies,"

Holly assured her. "If we can't make it to the hospital, he can deliver your baby for you. Can't you, Ben?"

"Sure thing. A hospital would be preferable, but either way you're in good hands. Now just lay back and relax. Remember to breathe. Slow, deep, cleansing breaths."

The drive along the straight stretch of road through the valley was a quicker one than the slow, inching speed the curvy mountain pass had required. "It should just be a few more minutes," Ben said, trying to encourage the woman, who had just let out a loud scream as a contraction gripped her body.

"I'm okay," Mary assured us from the back. "Sorry about the scream, but the pain has passed. There should be a driveway on the left no more than a mile ahead."

"I think I see it." Holly pointed to a narrow drive that, thankfully, someone had plowed. There was a set of fresh tire tracks leading off the main road onto the drive. "It looks like someone's here. I see fresh tire tracks."

Ben turned carefully into the drive and made his way toward the brightly lit house. There were two trucks in front of the building. Ben parked as close to the front door as he could, then went around back to help Mary out.

"Can I help you?" an elderly man asked from the front door.

"I'm Ben Holiday. We came across a woman whose vehicle was stuck in a ditch just down the road a bit. Her name is Mary and she's in labor. We need to get her inside and call the hospital."

"Bring her in. I'll just run and put some fresh sheets on the bed."

Ben and Holly helped Mary into the warm living room of the small log cabin. A crackling fire danced in the old stone fireplace and a small but brightly lit tree graced the corner of the room near the compact kitchen. Soft jazz played on a stereo, giving the room a cozy and relaxed feel.

"I'm afraid the phone lines are down, but I have a truck with a plow on the front," the man explained as he walked into the living room from the bedroom that opened just off it. "The snow's pretty much stopped in the past half hour, so I think I can make it into town without too much trouble. Bed has fresh sheets, and there are extra blankets in the dresser near the window. You folks just settle our little mother in and make her as comfortable as you can and I'll be back quick as possible."

"Thank you, Mr. . . . ?" Holly paused.

"Just call me Pop. Everyone does. There are clean towels in the bathroom closet and pans to heat water under the stove if you need them. Help yourself to whatever you need. I'll be back in a jiffy."

Pop whistled for his dog, a small border collie that had been watching the commotion from his vantage point on the sofa, and, pulling his collar up around his ears, trudged into the deep snow toward his plow and the promise of help.

Holly settled Mary into the large, soft bed as Ben rummaged around for the supplies they might potentially need if Mary's baby decided to make his appearance before Pop's return.

"His name is Michael," Mary volunteered as Holly tucked a warm comforter around her large, round belly. "After my dad. He died two years ago, but I wanted his name to live on."

"That's nice. Michael's a good name. I think it's nice when parents give their children names with special meaning. A lot of people these days just try to come up with the silliest name they can think of. I'm sure your dad would be proud to pass his name on to his grandson."

"Do you and Ben have any children?" Mary asked.

"No, Ben's just a friend. We're not married."

"Oh, I thought I sensed a more intimate connection between you. You seem to work really well together, like people who have been together a long time."

"Actually, I met him less than a week ago." Holly looked around the room and tried to decide if there was anything else she should be doing. Nothing came to mind, but standing around didn't seem quite right either.

"So what are you doing out in the middle of nowhere in one of the biggest storms we've had in a long time with a man you only met a week ago?" Mary asked.

"It's a very long and very complicated story."

"I could use a distraction right about now," Mary said encouragingly. "Why don't you tell me your story, if you don't mind, that is? It'll help take my mind off the pain of the contractions."

"Sure, why not?" Holly found a chair and sat down next to the bed. Holding her hand, she told her about the road trip, leaving out any hint of her growing feelings for Ben. Meanwhile, Ben busied himself in the main part of the cabin, stopping to check in on his patient and fill in a few missing details in Holly's rendition as he worked.

The hours passed slowly as Mary's contractions increased in both timing and intensity. Mary tried to keep up a brave front, but Holly could sense her increasing fear as Michael's imminent birth became more and more apparent.

"You better get Ben." Mary groaned as a particularly hard contraction gripped her body.

"Okay, now I want you to push," Ben instructed Mary a half hour later, when Michael made it clear he wasn't going to wait for Pop's return. "Just a little more; we're almost there."

"Oh my God, I see his head," Holly breathed.

"Now, I want you to stop pushing while I free up his shoulders. Pant if you feel the need to push, but don't actually push until I tell you to."

"Okay."

Ben maneuvered the baby into position and, supporting his head, told Mary to push one final time. Michael came sliding out into Ben's hands as Mary and Holly both sobbed with joy and relief.

"He's so beautiful. And so small." Holly stared at him with wonder.

"I want to see." Mary tried to sit up.

"Let me cut the cord and I'll bring him to you." Ben cut the cord, wiped the placenta from the baby's face, and wrapped him in a soft towel he had found in the bathroom.

Tears streamed down Mary's face as she held her baby for the first time. "He's perfect."

"I think I hear sirens." Holly walked over to the window and looked out. "It seems the cavalry has arrived."

A few minutes later, Pop walked in with the county snowplow driver and a pair of paramedics from the next town.

"Well, I'll be. Looks like we were too late after all." Pop ran a gnarled finger over the baby's soft blond hair.

"We'd like to take you back to town, ma'am. You and the baby should be checked out by a doctor," one of the young paramedics said.

"Of course." Mary passed the baby to Holly. "Can you hold him while I get dressed and clean up a bit?"

Holly gently rocked Michael as she stared at his angelic face and wondered for the first time if her own mother had held her in such a way. When she was five, Aunt Meg had told her that her mother had died in the accident when she was only days old. She'd never wondered about her much after that, never stopped to consider whether she had been wanted, cherished, loved. Had her own mother held her in her arms and wondered at the miracle of new life? Had she rocked her and sung to her and kissed her tiny forehead?

For the first time ever, Holly wondered what name her own mother had given her. Had she been named after a beloved relative or the latest pop star or a popular beverage? Had she spent months dreaming of her, planning for her, loving her? Or had she planned to give her away all along?

"I thought we'd follow the ambulance into town and spend the night there." Ben interrupted her thoughts. "That way, if it snows some more tonight, we'll be that much closer to the interstate."

"Okay. Just let me say good-bye to Pop." Holly handed Michael to Ben and went in search of their gracious host.

Chapter 8

Tuesday, December 3

"Good morning, sleepyhead." Ben kissed Holly on the forehead and set a steaming cup of coffee and a warm croissant on the night table next to her.

"What time is it?" Holly yawned.

"Almost eleven o'clock."

"Really? Why didn't you wake me?"

"You were exhausted. I wanted you to get some sleep."

"But now we'll never make it to Gardiner today."

"Au contraire. The storm has cleared up and we have a beautiful, sunny day. I called the highway patrol, and all roads between here and Gardiner are clear and open. And I called Lilly Walton and made an appointment to visit with her later this afternoon. She's expecting us at around three o'clock, which should give you time to shower, and we can have some lunch before we hit the road."

"You're a god." Holly took an appreciative sip of her coffee. "You've handled everything while I snored away. I feel a little guilty."

"Don't. You needed some rest. Now, hop in the shower and I'll meet you in the diner next door in forty-five minutes."

After Ben left, Holly stripped off her flannel pj's and stood looking at her naked frame in the full-length mirror on the back of the bathroom door. She touched a hand to her flat stomach and imagined herself pregnant.

Holly had spent her whole life trying to make something of herself, to build a career, to give her name texture and meaning. Never once in her twenty-seven years had she wondered what it would be like to have a houseful of kids. Not until she met Ben, that is. She'd always thought Noel a little nuts: four kids in ten years. Until she watched the miracle of birth, witnessed Mary's joy, and held Michael in her arms, she'd never understood the divine purpose and fulfillment that came from bringing new life into the world.

Holly tried to picture New York. She tried to care about the fact that her column might be syndicated. She tried to imagine how gratified and successful she'd feel when she was promoted and given a big corner office. She tried to imagine the upscale apartment and fancy sports car she'd finally be able to afford. But all she could picture was a baby bump and the promise of new life.

Her cell phone rang as she was grabbing her bag to head downstairs. She considered letting it go through to voice mail, but the caller ID indicated that it was Madison.

"Holly, I'm glad I caught you," Madison said, jumping right in. "I have a buyer interested in Meg's land."

"Noel told me. Must be a big family to need all those bedrooms."

"Actually," Madison paused, "the buyer isn't interested in the house. In fact, he plans to tear it down. It's the land he has his eye on."

Holly frowned. "He doesn't want the house?"

"No. He's planning to build an office complex on the property. Thirty acres close to town, yet far enough off the beaten path to avoid zoning issues. I think we can get a very nice price."

Holly thought of the big white house with the noisy heater and leaky roof. She thought of the dozens of kids who had lived within its walls, and the huge family-style meals they'd shared at the dining table that comfortably sat twenty. She thought of the early morning squabbles as a dozen kids jockeyed for position to use one of the three bathrooms.

"Maybe even enough to put a nice down payment on an apartment in the city," Madison added when Holly didn't answer.

"I'm going to have to think about it. Go ahead and write up an offer and e-mail it to me. I'm on the road, so I might not be able to get back to you for a couple of days."

"No problem. The buyer is an out-of-town investor, so it'll probably take me a couple of days to get documents filled out anyway."

"Right on time," Ben congratulated her as she walked into the diner ten minutes later at exactly eleven thirty-eight.

"I'm starving. I just realized that we haven't eaten since breakfast yesterday."

"I talked to the waitress while you were getting ready. This place is known for its homemade soups and thick sandwiches on freshly baked bread. Today's special is chicken noodle soup and a ham sandwich."

"Sounds perfect."

"Good, because I already ordered one for both of us. I figured it would speed up the process a little, and I know you're anxious to get on the road."

"I am. I know it's a long shot, but I really hope Lilly Walton can provide us with the next clue we need in our journey. Have you thought at all about what our next move might be if she doesn't know anything?"

Ben motioned to the waitress for a refill on his coffee. "I have a buddy checking to see if he can find out the names and whereabouts of the detectives who originally investigated the accident. It's a long shot, but maybe we can find a lead they missed if we can pick their brains a little."

"Do you think they're still around? It's been a long time," Holly pointed out.

"I don't know. Maybe."

Lilly Walton lived on a large ranch at the end of a very long drive off an isolated back road near Gardiner. She was a tiny woman, no more than five feet at most, with a huge personality that filled the space of ten people.

"Come in, come in." Lilly reached up and hugged Holly and Ben in turn. "Oh, I am so glad to meet you. It's not often I have company these days. Have a seat and I'll get us some tea. Or would you prefer scotch? I like a little scotch every now and then."

"Tea will be fine." Holly smiled at the energetic woman as she fluttered around the room, straightening perfectly straight throw pillows and swatting at imaginary dust on the shiny coffee table.

"Your young man here said you were looking for information that might help you track down your missing family." Lilly poured tea from the perfectly polished silver teapot into bright white china cups. She set the cups on a silver tray next to white ceramic cream and sugar servers, then brought the whole thing over to the coffee table, in front of the sofa on which they were sitting.

"Yes, ma'am." Holly picked up her teacup and took a sip. "It seems that the vehicle in which I was found belonged to a neighbor you used to have, Carl Langley."

"Whatever were you doing in that old coot's rattletrap of a vehicle? I didn't even know that dilapidated thing ran."

"I'm not sure." Holly accepted one of the home-baked cookies Lilly offered her. "The car had been in an accident and the people I was with were burned beyond recognition. Their identities have never been discovered. Actually, neither has mine."

"Oh, dear," the woman tsk-tsked. "That is quite a tragedy."

"I'm hoping to find out exactly what happened. I know it was a long time ago—twenty-seven years, to be exact—but I thought maybe you could tell me something, anything, about Mr. Langley or the couple that might help me in my search."

"Holly was found in Mr. Langley's vehicle on December 22," Ben explained. "Police reports from the initial investigation indicate that Mr. Langley was found dead by you on December 24 of that same year."

"Yes, I remember." Lilly refilled everyone's cup from the silver pot before settling in to tell her story. "I had gone over to Carl's to bring him a Christmas cake. He was an ornery cuss, but he was alone, and I always felt sorry for him during the holidays. I found him on the floor. It looked like he had been dead for at least a couple of days."

"Can you remember anything else? Anything that seemed out of the ordinary?" Ben asked.

"The police said that Carl had died from a heart attack. That he had been alone and had simply fallen to the floor. I remember noticing that the bed had been stripped. I looked around while I waited for the police but found no evidence of the discarded bed linens."

"That's strange." Holly sat forward. "Did you tell all of this to the police?"

"I did. They said that their investigation didn't uncover any evidence of the missing bedsheets, but that missing sheets didn't necessarily indicate foul play. The medical examiner confirmed that Carl died of a heart attack, and there was no evidence of anyone else being in the house."

"Did you happen to notice if his car was there?" Ben inquired.

"I can't say that I remember one way or the other," Lilly answered. "It's been a long time, and I wasn't really looking for clues at the time."

"Our investigation seems to indicate the couple driving Mr. Langley's vehicle were Hispanic, and not Holly's biological parents," Ben informed her. "A woman we met in town, Mrs. Trundle, indicated that Mr. Langley had a Hispanic couple who sometimes helped him out with the shopping and chores. Can you tell us who that couple was?"

"Do you think they had something to do with Carl's death?"

"Not necessarily. If Carl did indeed die of natural causes, we'd have no reason to suspect them of any wrongdoing. We're curious about how the couple ended up with Mr. Langley's car, though."

"You think the couple in the car was the same couple that used to help Carl out?"

"Possibly," Ben confirmed. "Although at this point there's no way to tell. All we know for certain is that the couple that perished in the accident was Hispanic."

Lilly stopped to consider what Ben had told her. "I do remember a couple who used to help out old Carl. Nice people. I hope it wasn't them. I can't say that I remember their names. The man had a real odd name. Something biblical, like Zechariah or Jedediah. Not at all a typical Hispanic name."

"Do you know of anyone who might remember his name? Or maybe his wife's name?" Holly asked hopefully.

"Can't say that I do. They only came around about once a week or so, and that was a long time ago. I know the wife used to bring Carl groceries, but I think she brought the supplies with her most weeks. Sure wish I could remember that old guy's name." Lilly tapped her chin with her index finger while she thought. "There was a fire about thirty years ago that threatened the whole town. Everyone for miles around turned out to help fight it," Lilly said. "The local paper printed the names of everyone who helped. If his name was listed, I'm sure I'd recognize it. I think I have a copy of the article in the attic. If you could give me a hand, young man?"

Lilly pointed Ben and Holly to a narrow set of steep stairs that led to a small doorway. The attic was dark and musty. It was piled high with overflowing boxes, old furniture, and stacks of magazines and newspapers.

"Excuse the mess. My family has lived in this house for three generations and you do tend to collect quite a bit of clutter during that amount of time. I think the article I'm looking for is over here."

Lilly made her way around the souvenirs from her family's past until she found the box she was looking for. "Here it is." She held up the yellowed newspaper article. "It's quite a list. If it weren't for the sacrifice and supreme effort of everyone on this list, this house wouldn't be here today. Let's see now."

Lilly perched her glasses on the tip of her nose and started to read. "My, my. So many of these people have since passed on. I hadn't realized. The years fly by faster than you'll ever know. Here we are: Nehemiah Sanchez of Livingston, Montana."

"Is Livingston far from here?" Holly asked.

"'Bout sixty miles."

"Thank you so much for your help." Holly took Lilly's hands in her own. "It must be wonderful to live in such a beautiful home, rich with the history of those who came before you. I can't even imagine how wonderful it must be to feel so firmly planted in your roots. I hope I can find even a little piece of mine."

"You let me know how everything turns out. Let's go back downstairs and I'll pack you some sandwiches for the road. I hope you find your answers."

"What now?" Holly asked when they'd returned to the car.

"I'd like to get my hands on the coroner's report, as well as the police report from the time of Carl's death," Ben said.

"How are we going to get a look at the reports?" Holly wondered.

"I suggest we start by asking."

A half hour later, Ben and Holly wandered into the local sheriff's office. It was small, with a single person in attendance.

"Can I help you?" the young woman asked.

"Yes. My name is Ben Holiday. I'm a private investigator." Ben showed the woman his credentials. "I'm here doing research on a cold case from twenty-seven years ago. I'd like to take a look at some of your files, if I may."

"I don't know." The woman hesitated. "You should check with the sheriff when he gets back."

"I'm afraid we're in a bit of a hurry. You can call Special Agent Griswold at the Federal Bureau of Investigation if you want to confirm my interest in this case."

"No, that's okay. All the files over five years old are in the back room. I'm afraid it's kind of a mess. The file boxes are marked on the outside with the date of the records contained inside."

"Thank you. Hopefully we won't be long."

The woman showed Ben and Holly to the back room. The file boxes were stacked from floor to ceiling in no apparent order.

"Wow. She wasn't kidding about the mess," Holly grumbled. "By the way, what would you have done if the woman had decided to check out your reference at the FBI?"

"Nothing. Roy would have covered for me. He's helped me out before."

"It really pays to have friends in high places."

"It does. You start at the other side of the room near the window. I'll start here."

After more than an hour of searching, Holly finally found a box that had files from the year she was born. "Over here."

Ben took the box over to a makeshift counter and opened the lid. "Here we are: Carl Langley."

He pulled the file from the box and read through the attached pages. "It doesn't look like the local police did much of an investigation at all. Lilly's report of the missing bedsheets is here, followed by a note that just says, 'nothing found.' The coroner's report isn't much better. The cause of death is just listed as natural, and the file indicates that no autopsy was performed."

"Is there anything else?"

"Not really. Seems pretty cut and dried." Ben closed the file.

"So now what?"

"Let's see if we can track down Nehemiah Sanchez."

"How do we do that?" Holly asked.

"We'll start with the local newspaper."

A search of the archives of the local newspaper produced the wedding announcement of Nehemiah Sanchez and Monica Rodriguez from almost forty years earlier. The names of the wedding party included Jarod Long, who served as best man, and the bride's sister, Rosa, who served as matron of honor. A subsequent search of a local telephone directory produced a current number for Jarod Long.

"Mr. Long," Ben introduced himself over the phone a few minutes later, "I'm a private investigator researching a missing person case. I was hoping to speak with Nehemiah Sanchez about it. I'm told you know Mr. Sanchez and was hoping you could give me his contact information."

"Nehemiah left town over twenty-five years ago. I have no idea where he went. I know the old man he was working for passed away, so I guess he just moved on, looking for work."

"You were friends. Didn't it seem odd to you that he didn't tell you where he was going?" Ben asked.

"Seemed odd at the time, but he grew to be pretty reclusive toward the end. A couple of weeks after he disappeared, his wife's sister, Rosa, came and packed up their stuff. She might know where they ended up. She used to live up north. I can get you the last address I have for her."

"That would be great." Ben motioned for Holly to get him a pen and something to write on. "Okay, thank you. You've been a big help."

"So?" Holly asked.

"He said Nehemiah moved on shortly after Carl Langley's death. He doesn't know where he went, but he gave me the last address for Monica's sister. She lived in a town about a hundred and fifty miles north of here. It's getting late. Let's find a place to stay and we'll head out there in the morning."

"Maybe we could try calling her."

"I think in this particular case it might be best to question her in person. If she still lives in the area, that is. It seems like Nehemiah took off under pretty odd circumstances, so she might not be forthcoming with any information about his whereabouts. I think we'll have a better chance of getting something out of her if we talk to her face-to-face."

"I'm sure you're right. Jessica just left me a message saying she forwarded everything I'll need to write this week's column, so I guess I should get that wrapped up and out of the way."

"Bozeman's just down the highway a bit. We should be able to find a place to stay there. What are you writing about this week?"

"Honestly, I'm not even sure. Before I left for this trip, Jessica and I had several different projects we were working on. With the holiday last week, I can't imagine she's made much progress on any of them, but her message said she had enough information to answer two of the letters. I'm just not sure which two. I'll call her after we get checked in and see what still needs to be done."

Chapter 9

Wednesday, December 4

The next morning, the pair headed north in what they hoped would be the answer to at least part of the puzzle. A quick search of the telephone directory told them that Rosa Rodriguez not only still lived in town but also, apparently, had never married, as evidenced by the use of her maiden name.

"Maybe we should get some lunch before we head over to Rosa's," Ben suggested. "I'm starving, and if Rosa does know something, we might be in for a lengthy conversation."

Holly nodded.

The place was a pretty little village with small, well-kept houses and a festively decorated downtown with a single café. Ben and Holly parked along the street and went inside. Although the building was run-down on the outside, inside it was warm and inviting, with locals sharing long, family-style tables while eating freshly made sandwiches and sharing the latest local gossip.

"Sarah," a buxom waitress greeted them. She hugged Holly. "You're back early. Your mama said you weren't due home for another week at least."

"I'm sorry, but my name is Holly, not Sarah," Holly corrected the woman, who still held her captive in an enormous bear hug.

"Oh, Sarah, you always were such a kidder. I sure have missed your sunny face around here. I was just telling Louis how good it would be to have you home for a few weeks."

"No, seriously. My name is Holly." Holly reached in her purse, grabbed her wallet, and pulled out her driver's license. "See, Holly Thompson."

"Well, I'll be. I swear, you're the spittin' image of our Sarah. Although now that I think about it, the last time she was home she had cut her hair short. Still," the woman looked shocked, "except for the hair, you could be twins. Are you sure you're not Sarah playing a trick on old Marge?"

"No, ma'am. I'm really not Sarah. I'd love to meet her, though. It'd be fun to actually talk to my double." Holly tried to sound nonchalant. "Can you tell me where I can find her?"

"She's a student at the university in Houston. Working on her Phd. Smart little thing, and such a sweetheart. The whole town has missed her since she's been gone. She should be back for Christmas. Maybe you could meet her then. In the meantime, you'll have to introduce yourself to her mama, Rosa Rodriguez. I can give you her address, although she won't be back from her trip to Billings for another four or five days. If you're still around, I'm sure she'd get a real kick out of meeting her daughter's virtual twin. Now sit down and let me get you some lunch."

Holly just stared at Ben, who hadn't said a word since they'd walked into the café. He took her arm and led her to a booth.

"Sarah has to be my sister," Holly whispered as the waitress went to get them some menus.

"I know," Ben whispered back.

"I don't think I can eat. I feel like I'm going to pass out."

"Just order something small."

"Here you go." Marge set menus in front of them. "The roast beef sandwiches are to die for."

"Thank you." Holly hoped she didn't look as stunned as she felt.

She took a look at the menu as other patrons in the café stared at her, commenting among themselves. Holly figured this was what a celebrity must feel like every time she went out in public. Every ounce of self-preservation she possessed demanded that she get up and flee the room in order to avoid the extreme level of scrutiny of dozens of pairs of eyes. Ben must have sensed her discomfort because he placed his hand on her arm and squeezed it in a demonstration of support.

"Have you decided?" Marge asked.

"I'll just have a salad," Holly said. "A small one."

"And I'll have a roast beef sandwich," Ben added.

"It looks like the weather should be nice the next few days," Ben said, introducing a neutral topic as Marge stepped away. "I saw on the news that the East Coast is getting slammed with a series of storms."

"I guess it's a good thing we aren't home." Holly knew their conversation would bore anyone who might be listening in. "Maybe I'll call Jessica and get the latest. You know how these forecasters are. They call for two feet and we get two inches."

"I talked to my mom earlier and she said it's snowing pretty hard."

Marge set the salad and sandwich on the table and refilled their glasses of water.

"You folks out this way on vacation?" she asked.

"Business," Ben answered.

"Oh, what kind of business?"

"Sales." Ben took a bite of his sandwich, eliminating the possibility of further conversation.

"Will you be in the area long?" Marge asked Holly, who was poking at her salad.

"Um, we're not sure. This is really good dressing," she said, changing the subject. "Do you think I can get a little more?"

"Sure thing." Marge walked away.

Ben and Holly ate quickly and left a big tip. They hated to be rude, but Holly thought she might explode if they didn't get away from staring eyes and listening ears to someplace they could talk.

"Oh my God, oh my God, oh my God," Holly said the minute they left the restaurant.

Ben laughed.

"When we began this journey, I hoped I had a sister somewhere in the world, but to be honest, I don't think I really let myself believe it. Now that it looks like it might be a reality, I find that I'm both excited and nervous. What should we do now?"

"We could wait until Rosa comes home in four or five days, or we could head to Houston," Ben said. "I'd suggest calling Sarah, but under the circumstances, I think a face-to-face meeting is called for."

"Let's go to Houston." Holly turned and walked toward the car. "How long do you think it'll take?"

"If we drive straight through and don't run into any more bad weather, we should be there by Saturday evening."

"And you're really committed to this no-flying thing?"

"'Fraid so."

"Okay, let's go."

"Ben," Holly said several hours later, as they zipped along the highway toward Texas, "do you think Sarah will be glad to see me? I mean, something strange happened to us when we were babies, something beyond a normal adoption. If things had been aboveboard, someone would have reported me, and the couple I was riding with, as missing, and the police would have figured things out twenty-seven years ago. I don't know what happened to our real mother, or why Sarah was with Rosa while I was with Nehemiah and Monica, but Sarah was raised by a real adoptive mother in a real home and might not appreciate having her whole life turned upside down."

"If it were you, wouldn't you want to know the truth?" Ben asked as they merged onto the highway.

"I don't know. I guess. I'm not sure."

"Do you want to stop the investigation?" Ben asked. "We can turn the car around and head to Moosehead if you want."

Holly hesitated. "No, I need to know. I just hope I don't destroy my sister's life in the process."

"I'll make some calls when we stop for the night to see what I can find out about Sarah and her adoption. Maybe things are more on the up and up than we think."

They stopped driving earlier than they had originally planned so Ben could make his calls before it got to be too late on the East Coast. The snail's pace of the trip was beginning to grate on Holly's nerves, but, as Ben had reminded her many times in the past week, road-trip etiquette required a much more relaxed and easygoing approach to obstacles than was within the parameters of Holly's type A personality.

"Did you find out anything?" Holly asked as they settled into a booth at a small diner.

"A little." Ben unfolded his napkin and placed it in his lap. "There are a few callbacks I'm still waiting for. Sarah Rodriguez is in her final year of her doctorate program in theoretical physics. She's becoming quite renowned in her field; you should be proud of her."

"I am, and I haven't even met her."

"There's no record of an adoption of a baby girl by Rosa Rodriguez who, as we guessed, never married."

"So how did Sarah come to be with her?"

"That I don't know. I'm looking for a copy of a birth certificate. She must have had some kind of records in order to enroll in school. So far, I haven't found anything, but I have people checking."

"Anything else?"

"I found a copy of Sarah's driver's license. Her birthday is listed as May 22."

"So she can't be my sister," Holly concluded.

"Not necessarily. If Rosa had counterfeited documents, she could have listed the birth date as anything she wanted."

"But why make her so much older than she really is?"

"Chances are, the presence of a birth certificate didn't become an issue until Sarah was ready to enter the school system. With a December birthday, she would have had to wait a whole year to enter kindergarten. She's obviously a very bright girl;

maybe Rosa wanted to start her early, so when she had the documents forged, she moved up her birth date."

"Poor Sarah. Not only am I about to tell her that her mother is a liar, but that she's not even the age she thinks she is."

"It'll be okay. We'll figure it out."

"I've been so focused on finding my sister and the truth about my past that I've never stopped to think how it might affect the other people involved. Am I doing the right thing or am I just being selfish?"

"What do you think?" Ben asked.

"Honestly, I'm not sure."

"I'll support whatever you decide to do. For now, though, let's order dinner and get a good night's rest. Tomorrow we'll see what we can find out and take it from there."

"I doubt I'll be able to sleep. I feel like my head's going to explode. I almost find myself wishing I hadn't finished this week's column last night. I suppose I could read the other letters Jessica sent, but I doubt I'd really be able to do any of them justice at this point."

"What you need is a diversion."

"Diversion?"

"I play a mean game of gin rummy," Ben offered.

Playing gin with Ben turned out to be fun and more distracting than Holly had first anticipated. He was funny and playful, and surprisingly romantic to boot. Somehow, by the end of their final game, they ended up in a pillow fight that left them entangled on the floor, laughing until their sides hurt.

"Uncle," Holly yelled when she thought she could laugh no more. "I give up. You win."

Ben stopped laughing. He caressed her cheek as he brushed her hair from her face. "Then the victor claims his prize." With that, he claimed her lips in a kiss that was anything but brotherly.

He lifted his head to look into her eyes. "I'm sorry. I shouldn't have done that."

Holly smiled shyly. "I didn't mind."

"I care about you, Holly. More than I ought to."

"I care about you, too, Ben. A lot."

"The thing is that I made a promise to Meg, and to you. I want to help you find your answers, your truth. This journey we've embarked on is a hugely emotional one for you, for both of us. If we take our relationship to the next level, I'm afraid that things could become even more complicated than they already are."

"But Ben . . ."

"Besides," Ben interrupted, "when we make love, I want it to be more than just a diversion. I want it to be a decision, a commitment. One that is pure and uncluttered by a myriad of emotions brought on by outside factors." Ben kissed her on the forehead. "Get some sleep. We need to get an early start tomorrow."

Ben walked through the door connecting their two rooms and closed it behind him.

Chapter 10

Thursday, December 5

"Look at that kid hitchhiking on the side of the road." Holly pointed to a young boy, who couldn't be more than ten, standing with his thumb out, a tattered bag and filthy dog at his side, as they drove along an access road after stopping to get gas.

Ben pulled over. "We'd better check it out."

"Hey, mister. You headed south?" the paper-thin boy, with curly blond hair, bright blue eyes, and dirt-streaked cheeks asked.

"We are."

"Can you give us a ride to Phoenix?"

"Phoenix is quite a ways for someone so young to be traveling by himself," Ben pointed out.

"I'm not so young." The boy tried to stand taller. "Just small for my age. Besides, I'm not alone, I'm with Dusty here. Now can I have that ride or not?"

"Where are your parents?" Ben asked.

"Dead."

Ben hesitated. "I see. Is there someone you're staying with? Someone who is responsible for you?"

"I can take care of myself. I don't need no one."

Ben hesitated before continuing. "Why do you want to go to Phoenix?"

"Look, mister, my business is my business. Now, are you going to give us a ride or not?" The frightened child's eyes darted around, as if assessing the easiest escape route.

"What's your name?" Ben asked.

"Bobby."

"Bobby what?"

"Just Bobby."

"Okay, Just Bobby. Jump in. Phoenix is a little out of our way, but we'll see what we can do."

"Dusty, too?"

"Sure, why not? I'll open the back. He can ride in the cargo area."

Bobby loaded Dusty into the back, climbed into the backseat, and promptly fell asleep.

"Do you think he's a runaway?" Holly whispered.

"Probably."

"Should we call the police or something? His parents must be frantic. Although," Holly looked around at the desolate landscape, "there really isn't much out here. Where do you think he came from?"

"I have no idea. When we stop, I'll call a buddy of mine and have him check out the local missing-persons reports. This kid has obviously been on the streets for a while. I'm afraid if we spook him, he'll just take off again. At least I know he's safe with us."

"He could definitely use a bath," Holly said, wrinkling her nose. "Dusty, too. And probably a good meal."

"I hate to suggest this, but I think we should stop early tonight. We'll feed Bobby and Dusty and get them baths, and I can make my calls before we get too far away from where we found him."

"Okay. As much as all the delays are making me nuts, I agree we need to find out who this boy is and where he belongs. Aunt Meg took in a couple of runaways over the years. Most had a good reason to run. I wonder what his is."

"I wish I knew."

Ben consulted the map on his phone and changed direction. "Guess this will set us back a few days. I figure Phoenix is about a day and a half from here, and Houston will be another day and a half or so.

"That's okay," Holly assured him. "No way I'm leaving that little guy to fend for himself."

Ben found a motel in the next town. Each of the connecting rooms had two double beds and a large, round table. Ben gave Bobby and Dusty baths while Holly went in search of a healthy meal for the four of them. After returning to the motel, she stood at the connecting door, listening and watching as man and boy bonded over common ground.

"Don't see why I had to take no bath," Bobby complained.

"Because you smelled like my fishing boat at the end of a long weekend," Ben said.

"You have a boat?"

"I do."

"Me and Dusty like to fish. Maybe you could take us sometime."

"Maybe. After we get you settled in Phoenix. Who did you say you were going to visit?" Ben asked as he combed the little boy's hair back away from his face.

"I didn't."

"I see." Ben stood back to consider his handiwork. "Much improved."

"Do you have any kids?" Bobby wondered.

"No. You?"

"No, silly." Bobby laughed. "I *am* a kid."

Ben looked up and noticed Holly standing in the doorway. "It looks like Holly's back with food. Why don't you and Dusty go on over to her room and eat while I make a few phone calls?"

"Aren't you eatin'?"

"Yeah, after I make my calls."

"Okay. Come on, Dusty." Bobby got up from his spot in front of the television and walked through the connecting door into Holly's room and, probably, the first meal he'd had in days.

"I hope you like hamburgers." Holly set a burger, fries, and a carton of milk in front of the freshly scrubbed youth.

"Did you get ketchup?"

"I did." Holly tossed several packets of ketchup across the table. "I also got mustard, mayonnaise, and a couple of extra patties for Dusty. And for dessert"— Bobby stopped shoveling food into his mouth long enough to look up expectantly—"fruit. Apples and bananas."

"Fruit's not dessert," Bobby complained.

"I thought we needed to add something nutritional to the meal. Growing boys need their fruit and veggies."

"You sound like my mom."

Holly paused. "Your mom sounds like a smart woman. I bet she's missing you something awful."

Bobby hastily wiped a tear that was just forming in the corner of his eye. "She died a few months ago. Car crash. My dad, too."

Holly placed her hand over Bobby's forearm, careful not to spook him. "I'm so sorry. You must miss them terribly."

"Yeah," Bobby whispered.

"Do you have any brothers or sisters?" Holly asked.

Bobby hesitated. He started to speak, then stopped. "Hey, what's with all the questions?"

"Sorry. I wasn't trying to pry. I just wanted to get to know you a little better. I figured if we were going to be traveling together for the next couple of days, we should know a little about each other."

"Well, I don't want to talk no more. Can we turn on the TV? *Power Rangers* was on channel twenty-seven."

"Sure. I love *Power Rangers.*"

"What'd you find out?" Holly asked several hours later, after Bobby and Dusty had been settled for the night in the second double bed in Ben's room.

"Nothing yet. I called a friend who is going to run a check for runaways and missing persons. I took Bobby's picture with my cell phone when he wasn't looking and forwarded it to him. He said he'd e-mail me anything he could find. We should know something by morning. In the meantime, we need to see if we can find out anything more about him. If we don't have any answers by morning, we'll continue toward Phoenix. It's a long drive; maybe he'll relax and spill something we can use to identify him."

"He said his parents were killed in an automobile accident a couple of months ago," Holly informed him.

"He might be lying. If he doesn't want us to try to find them, he might have made up the whole story."

"I don't think so. He was pretty choked up when he told me about it. Maybe he ended up in the foster-care system and he's running away from his foster home."

"Maybe, but where's he running to? Why Phoenix?" Ben ran his hand through his hair, fatigue evident on his face.

"I don't know. Did you look through his bag? There might be a clue inside."

"Yeah, while he was in the bathtub. Nothing in it but a change of clothes equally as dirty as the one he was wearing, a toothbrush and a tube of toothpaste, and a crumpled-up picture of a young girl. I doubt she's older than he is."

"A sister?"

"Maybe. There's a definite resemblance. Right now, I'm going to go out and see if there are any stores open where I can get him some new clothes. The ones he has have definitely seen better days. Will you keep an eye on him?" Ben asked.

"No problem. Poor little guy. I hope we find his family, and I hope they're worth finding. Not all families are, you know."

"Unfortunately, I do."

Chapter 11

Friday, December 6

Holly took Bobby to breakfast the next morning, while Ben checked in with his contact, Roy Griswold. Roy confirmed that no one of Bobby's description had been reported as a runaway or missing child, but he promised to keep looking, and Ben said he would check back with him when they stopped for lunch.

Holly sipped her coffee as Bobby ate a huge stack of pancakes at the diner down the street, complete with a double order of bacon on the side. The amount of food Bobby had ingested since they'd found him on the side of the road made Holly wonder how long before that he'd had a decent meal.

"You must have been hungry," Holly commented as he shoveled the food into his mouth.

"A little. Dusty's real hungry, though. Can we get something for him?"

"Sure. What do you think he'd like? I'll have the waitress make up a to-go box."

"He likes most anything. Maybe a steak and some eggs."

"A steak it is." Holly motioned for the waitress. "Have you had Dusty long?"

"No, not long. We sort of found each other. I was traveling south and he was, too, so we hooked up."

"He seems pretty committed to you." Holly handed Bobby a napkin to wipe syrup from his face. "He rarely leaves your side."

"What's committed?"

"Committed is like loyal," Holly explained. "Someone who will always be there for you, no matter what."

"I like that. People ought to be more committed to each other, like a dog. We'd have a lot less problems, don't you think?"

"Yes, I do." Holly smiled at the insightful little boy, who looked a lot younger than ten once they'd gotten all the dirt washed off of him. Her heart ached when she thought of him alone on the road. Whatever could have happened to him to make him set out on his own?

"Where's Ben?" Bobby asked after the waitress had come by to take their to-go order for Dusty.

"He had to make a few calls before we leave. He'll be back in a minute. Do you need to use the bathroom before we leave?"

"No, I'm good."

"Okay. I'll pay the check and pick up Dusty's steak; then we'll go find Ben."

Once they were on the road, Holly turned on the radio. A montage of Christmas carols filled the car with holiday cheer. "Do you have any plans for Christmas?" Holly asked Bobby.

"No. Christmas is dumb. Me and Dusty don't believe in Christmas." Holly wasn't surprised Bobby felt that way. A lot of her foster brothers and sisters had expressed the same sentiment over the years. After a few disappointments, kids tended to give up believing in magic.

"That's too bad. Christmas is such a special time, especially for children."

"What's so special about it?"

"Everything. I can remember how excited I'd get when I was your age. We'd spend an entire day decorating the outside of the old farmhouse. Not only did we put up outdoor lights but Aunt Meg had a life-size Santa and eight life-size reindeer that she'd position just so in front of a bright red sleigh. After we finished outdoors, we'd move inside and decorate every room with home-crafted decorations. Once the house was decked out in the finest holiday adornment, we'd all gather together to decorate the tree. Everyone got to help, but the youngest member of the household always got to put the star on the top. Aunt Meg would make cookies and we'd sing our favorite carols. As Christmas got closer, we'd make homemade gifts as we waited anxiously for Santa's arrival."

"There ain't no Santa. You're old, you oughtta know that." Bobby rolled his eyes.

"You're never too old for the magic of Christmas."

"That Christmas stuff is a bunch of crap. There may be a bunch of pretty lights and stuff, but parents still die, and kids are taken away from everything they love, only to be left alone to take care of themselves."

"I guess I see your point," Holly sympathized.

"I'm running a little low on gas." Ben changed the subject as Holly tried to discreetly wipe a tear from her cheek. "Maybe you could let Dusty out to stretch his legs while I fill the tank. There's an empty field across the street from the gas station. Be careful crossing."

Holly stood next to Ben as he pumped gas into the SUV. "Poor Bobby. He's all alone in the world, with no one but a dog to love him. At least I had Aunt Meg. Even though I was an orphan, not once did I ever feel alone. He must have someone who can take care of him. Grandparents, aunts, uncles?"

"Chances are he ended up in the foster-care system after his parents died. Not all foster homes are like Aunt Meg's. Some are really bad, but even in the best ones, it's hard not to feel isolated and alone. Nothing really belongs to you. Not your bed, not your toys, sometimes not even your clothes. Parents who aren't your own, no matter how nice they are, can feel like strangers who just want to boss you around."

"That's pretty insightful for someone who grew up in a large, loving family. How do you know how it feels to be a foster kid?" Holly asked.

"I guess I have a good imagination."

Holly waved at Bobby, who was throwing a stick for Dusty to fetch. "What are we going to do when we get to Phoenix? We can't just drop him off. He's so little. He needs someone to look after him."

"Don't worry; we'll be sure he's in good hands before we leave. Now, let's get Bobby and Dusty and head on down the road. Bobby's obviously running toward something. I doubt he randomly chose Phoenix as his destination. My guess is that he has someone there he cares about."

"I hope so. Maybe I'll pop into the mini-mart and get some snacks for the road. Both Bobby and Dusty seem to have bottomless pits for stomachs."

"Get nacho cheese chips." Ben handed her a twenty-dollar bill.

"I can pay for the snacks myself," Holly reminded him.

Ben didn't argue as he put his wallet away. "Maybe a Pepsi and some beef jerky while you're at it."

"Beef jerky? Really?" Holly grimaced.

"Learned a long time ago that there are certain things you do when you're on a road trip that you wouldn't do at other times. Eating beef jerky is one of them."

"Okay, if you say so." Holly fetched her purse from the car and turned toward the mini-mart

Two hours later, they stopped for lunch, and Ben went to check in with his contacts while Holly and Bobby got a table.

"Ben sure does have to make a lot of phone calls," Bobby observed as they perused the menu.

"I think he's just checking in with work," Holly offered as an excuse.

"My dad used to work a lot, too. I think it made my mom mad. Sometimes I'd hear them fighting about it after we went to bed."

"We? Do you have siblings? Brothers or sisters?"

Bobby hesitated. "Sisters. Two. Becky and Annie."

"And where are they?"

Bobby fidgeted in his seat, kicking the booth across from him as he slid down to hide behind his menu. "Staying with some relatives."

"I see, and why aren't you staying with them, too?"

"Didn't want to. I like being on my own."

"Don't you miss them? I have a sister. I've never even met her, and yet I still miss her."

Bobby set down his menu and looked across the table at Holly. "What do you mean, you never even met her?"

"We were separated shortly after we were born. I didn't even know she existed until a few days ago. But now that I know about her, I find myself missing her."

"Maybe you should go and see her," Bobby suggested.

"I am. In fact, that's where we were going when we picked you up. I'm a little scared, though."

"Scared? Why?"

"I guess I'm not sure she'll like me."

"Why wouldn't she like you? You're pretty nice, for a grown-up," he emphasized. "You're easy to talk to. I'll bet she misses you, too."

Holly smiled. "Thanks. I feel better. You're a pretty special young man."

Bobby blushed. "Can we order now? I'm starved."

"Sure. I think I'll have the chicken sandwich. I'll order one for Ben, too. What are you going to have?"

"The burger looks good, with extra pickles. And don't forget to get one for Dusty."

After they finished eating, Ben sent Bobby to walk Dusty in the field next door while he filled Holly in on what he had found out during his lunchtime phone call.

"I got some info on Bobby," Ben informed Holly. "His parents died four months ago. He was sent, along with his two sisters, to live with a grandmother.

After a couple of months, it became apparent that the grandmother was too old and frail to handle Bobby's bitterness and corresponding behavior problems. He was sent to live with an uncle, who lives about thirty miles west of where we picked him up. He's been there ever since. That is, until he ran away a week or so ago."

"Why didn't the uncle report him missing?" Holly wondered.

"He didn't even know he was gone. It seems he went on a gambling trip with some buddies and didn't know that Bobby took off."

"He left a ten-year-old alone for a week?"

"Apparently. And from what he said, I take it it's not the first time he's done it."

Holly shook her head in disgust. "So if the uncle didn't report him missing, how did you find him?"

"Bobby was assigned a case worker after his parents died. My buddy found his file in a social services database."

"And the sisters?" Holly wondered.

"They're still with the grandmother in Phoenix."

"So Bobby's going to Phoenix to find what's left of his family. How sad. What's going to happen to him now?"

"My contact wanted me to turn him over to social services, but I convinced him to let me take Bobby to Phoenix so I can speak to his grandmother. I'm hoping to convince her to let Bobby stay with her over the holidays in exchange for my promise to find him a permanent placement after the first of the year."

"Do you think she'll agree?"

"I don't know, but I plan to turn on the charm and try to convince her. I'll need to have a talk with

Bobby and get him to promise to behave himself while he's there."

"Do you think he will?" Holly asked.

"He might, if I promise him something he really wants in return."

"And what might that be?"

"A permanent home that will take both him and his sisters as a group."

"That's going to be hard to find," Holly pointed out.

"Yes, it is. But as they say, where there's a will, there's a way."

Bobby returned from walking Dusty and they loaded up the car and headed down the road again. Holly had always thought of the desert as a barren and desolate place, but she had to admit there was something enchanting about scenery that included nothing but mile upon mile of sagebrush and cacti. She leaned back as she took in the peace and serenity of the open road. It was too bad they were in a hurry, or she might have suggested they head toward the red rock of Sedona or the awesome majesty of the Grand Canyon.

"I had an interesting call from a buddy of mine while we were stopped for lunch." Ben turned his head slightly to look at Bobby.

"So?" Bobby didn't even look up.

"It seems your uncle finally figured out you ran away."

Bobby looked around frantically, as if seeking a way to escape the speeding vehicle. "Are you going to make me go back?"

"No. I don't think your uncle is the best guardian for you. I convinced my friend to let me take you to Phoenix to see your grandmother and sisters."

"She don't want me. She said I was corrigible."

"Do you mean incorrigible?"

"Yeah, I guess. She said she couldn't take care of me no more, so she sent me away. She let Becky and Annie stay, though. I really miss them, even if they are dumb girls."

"I have a plan that I think might let you and Becky and Annie be together, but I need your cooperation. Are you interested?"

"I guess. If Dusty can stay with us, too. What's cooperation?"

"Help. I'll need your help if my plan is to succeed."

"What do I have to do?"

Ben outlined his plan, detailing the boy's part in it. Bobby promised to mind his grandmother and not give her any lip, and Ben promised to call him every day to see how things were going. Now all that Ben had to do was get the grandmother's cooperation and, hardest of all, find a home that would take three children and a dog on a permanent basis.

The group stopped for the night at a clean but aging motel just off the interstate. They checked in and then headed over to the pool so Bobby could take a swim in the warm water.

"Can you believe we were stranded in a snowstorm a few days ago?" Holly sat on a chaise longue, her jeans rolled up above her knees.

"That's America for you. Drive long enough and you'll see a little bit of everything. Snow-covered mountains give way to open plains and sweeping vistas. Go a little farther south and you have red rock, deserts, huge canyons, and miles and miles of undeveloped desert. Ever been to the Louisiana bayou?"

"No, I can't say that I have. Does it look like it does in the movies? All dark and ominous?"

"Actually, it looks exactly like it does in the movies. We'll have to go sometime."

Holly smiled. "When you first told me that you were afraid to fly, I saw it as a handicap, but now I see that driving everywhere you want to go has exposed you to things that other people never experience. Although," she paused, "I've always wanted to go to Ireland. When I was a kid, it sounded so romantic. Rocky coastlines and haunted castles older than our country. Noel and I both swore we'd get married there, but in the end Noel got married in little old Moosehead."

"Watch me," Bobby called from the diving board. He ran to the end and did a cannonball into the water.

"Way to go." Holly waved to him as he proudly swam to the side of the pool near where they were sitting.

"So Ireland's still where you want to get married?" Ben asked when Bobby swam away.

"No, not really," she answered, but her voice said otherwise. "I mean, I'd still like to go there, but who knows if I'll ever get married? If I do, I guess I'll just have the wedding somewhere convenient."

"Convenient?"

Holly shrugged. "Probably the justice of the peace closest to wherever I happen to be living at the time. I know a lot of women want the fairy tale: a beautiful dress, a half dozen bridesmaids, and two or three hundred of their closest friends and relatives. In my opinion, that whole thing is highly overrated. One of the secretaries at the magazine got married last summer, and not only did she end up with an ulcer due to all the stress of planning the event but she was so exhausted from dealing with last-minute details that all she did was sleep during her very expensive European honeymoon."

"I suppose there's a halfway point between justice of the peace and migraine-inducing wedding spectacular," Ben pointed out. "Maybe a few family and close friends in a small chapel followed by a buffet dinner and dancing."

"That sounds like Noel's wedding. It was nice," Holly admitted. "Still, I remember the wedding insanity, with her worrying about whether she'd gain or lose weight so that her dress wouldn't fit, or the flowers would be all wrong, or the seating arrangement would cause World War III as complex personalities clashed due to undesirable proximity. When the band had to cancel at the last minute, poor Noel had a panic attack, and the whole thing was almost canceled. I sat with her the night before her wedding, holding her as she shattered into a mosaic of emotions, and vowed that I'd never put myself through such hell."

Ben frowned. "I think I'll change into my trunks and join Bobby."

"You brought some?"

"I always pack some when I travel. Even in colder climates, lots of places have indoor pools. Guess I should have reminded you to pack a suit. We can stop and get one for you when we go to dinner, if you want. We should have warm weather for the next few days at least."

"That sounds like a good idea. I think I saw a place next to that Mexican restaurant we passed. Maybe we can just eat there."

"A margarita sounds like just the thing," Ben agreed.

Ben joined Bobby in the pool, and Holly decided to use the time to call Jessica. Her assistant had really come through for her while she'd been gone. Not only had she screened and prioritized the letters she thought should be answered in her column but she'd completed all the research on the letters they'd already selected for the next couple of weeks. She figured she'd stay up late and write the actual columns using the research Jessica had done, keeping one step ahead of next week's deadline.

"Holly, I was hoping you'd call," Jessica said, answering on the first ring. "How goes the hunt?"

"I might have a sister," Holly answered, and then told Jessica everything that had happened during the past few days.

"Wow. That's so weird. Are you nervous about meeting her?"

"Extremely," Holly admitted. "But I'm also excited and hopeful. I can't even begin to explain all the emotions that are fluttering around inside me. I find it best not to dwell on it too much."

"Yeah, I get that."

"Do I have any messages?"

"A ton. I brought them home with me in case you called. Hang on while I get them."

Holly waited while Jessica retrieved her phone messages. "Derek has called three times this week. He said he left several messages on your cell, but you haven't called him back."

"I've been really busy and haven't had much chance to return calls. You told him I couldn't do lunch?"

"Yeah, but he's calling to reschedule. He seemed upset that you'd go out of town without telling him."

"Can you let him know I'll be unavailable until after the first of the year and we'll talk then?"

"He wants to know where you've gone."

"Tell him I'm doing research for my column. He's as big of a workaholic as I am; I'm sure he'll understand. Anything else?"

"Noel's called twice."

Holly sighed. "I really should check my messages. I'll call her as soon as we're done."

"I got the tickets for the benefit. And I talked to Kira and we made reservations for dinner after. The benefit is next Thursday. Do you think you'll be back?"

"No, probably not. Go ahead and find someone to give my tickets to, and pay for dinner for the group with the credit card I keep in my desk."

"Okay. Luckily, I haven't gotten around to setting you up with a date, so that won't be a problem. We do have a sort of biggish problem, however. Phillip wants to set up a meeting with the publishing group that's interested in syndicating your column next week."

Holly sighed. She really hoped that she'd have until after the new year, but syndicating her column was possibly the biggest thing that had ever happened to her. "I'll call him. I guess after we drop Bobby off and meet my sister, our journey will be wrapping up anyway."

"Bobby?" Jessica asked.

Holly explained about finding the little boy and his dog on the side of the road and their promise to return him to his grandmother and find him and his sisters a permanent place to live. "It's probably going to be an uphill battle to find someone who will take all three kids," Holly explained.

"You know what's sad?" Jessica said. "I talked with Amber Black, the woman who wrote to you under the name Thirteen Again." Jessica was referring to one of the letters they were working on, in which a woman complained that her mother was much too involved in her life. "When I first read the letter, I thought the mom, whose name turned out to be Veronica, was the bad guy, manipulating her daughter the way she had. The truth of the matter is, she's a lonely woman who just married off the youngest of her five children and desperately needs a sense of purpose in her life. She really thought she was helping Amber by managing the kids. I mean, I get why Amber wants her privacy, but I have to admit that after talking to Grandma, I feel really sorry for her. What we need is a program that matches up kids in need with women like Veronica, who are experiencing an empty nest but aren't quite ready for it."

"That's actually a really good idea," Holly complimented. "Do you think Veronica would be interested in being a foster parent?"

"Probably not, at least not right now, but maybe other women like her."

"I like the idea. Did we get Amber's situation straightened out?"

"Amber and her mom compromised. Mom takes a step back, and in return she gets to have the kids at her place one weekend a month, giving Amber the free time every single mom needs."

"Sounds like a good solution. Maybe you should be the advice columnist."

"No thanks. I'll stick to the research. Normally, I wouldn't have gotten as involved as I did, but with you being away, I figured I'd make a few phone calls on my own. Besides, the letter really got to me. My own mom can be a bit of a buttinsky, so I immediately identified with the poor woman. After looking at things from Veronica's side, though, I called my mom and agreed to let her come for an extended visit over the holidays. She's been asking to do it for a few years now, but I've always made up some excuse about too much work and stuff."

Holly couldn't imagine having a mother who wanted to spend time with her and making excuses not to, but she knew a lot of women who felt the way Jessica did.

When Holly finished talking with Jessica, she called Noel and left a message that she would get back to her at a later time.

"Phillip," Holly said, returning her final call, "how are things?"

"Good, but I need you back here. We're going to lose this syndication opportunity if we don't act on it."

"I told you before I left that I needed a leave of absence until after the first of the year," Holly reminded him.

"I know, and I told you I could only guarantee ten days. Things are moving faster than I expected. We need to get this sewn up as soon as possible. I'd like to set up a meeting for Monday."

"I'm halfway across the country," she said. "There's no way I can make it back for a meeting on Monday."

"You've heard they've invented those amazing flying machines, right?" Phillip teased.

"I realize that." Holly sighed. "Look, this deal is important to me, but I really can't get back that soon. Can you see if we can push the meeting back a few days at least?"

"I'll see what I can do."

Several hours later, the trio were walking through the little town, enjoying the colorful Christmas lights. "I noticed a movie theater down the block. It's still early. Anyone up for a show?" Ben offered. They'd finished eating and he had bought Holly the tiniest red bikini she'd ever seen. "My treat."

"Really?" Bobby exploded enthusiastically. "But what about Dusty?"

"He'll be okay in the motel room. We took him for a long walk when we first got here, and we can take him out again before bed."

"What's playing?"

"I have no idea, but as long as it's of the G variety, anything should be fine."

"My mom let me watch PG sometimes," Bobby said persuasively.

"We'll see."

After a rather long animated flick, the three weary travelers were more than ready to hit the sack. Ben unlocked the door to his room and stopped suddenly. "Everyone get back," he instructed them, pulling the door closed.

"What's wrong?" Holly asked.

"Someone broke into the room. I want you and Bobby to lock yourselves in the car while I check it out."

"Dusty!" Bobby screamed.

Ben walked Holly and Bobby to the car. He unlocked the doors and retrieved a gun that had been hidden in a compartment in the back.

"You have a gun?" Holly asked, surprised.

"I'm a private investigator. Of course I have a gun. Keep the doors locked until I get back."

They watched as Ben crept carefully back to the room and slowly opened the door. Holly could see him looking around, his firearm poised ahead of him, and entering the room.

"Where's Dusty?" Bobby cried. "He usually runs to the door as soon as we open it."

"I'm sure he's fine," Holly prayed.

"I need to get him." Bobby tried to open the door. "He might be hurt."

"No." Holly yelled louder than she should have, given the fear already evident in the little boy. "Ben said to wait."

Seconds ticked by seeming like hours. Bobby was crying hysterically, while Holly tried to offer comfort, though all she really wanted to do was join him. Finally, when Holly's nerves felt like they'd been stretched to the limit, Ben came out carrying a bleeding Dusty.

"Dusty!" Bobby screamed.

Holly opened the passenger door, and Ben placed Dusty in her lap.

"Is he dead?" Bobby cried.

"No. Whoever broke in hit him on the head, but he's breathing. I remember seeing a veterinary hospital down the road."

"Dusty," Bobby sobbed uncontrollably. "Please don't die. It's all my fault. Please be okay."

Ben sped down the street to the animal hospital, while Bobby sobbed and Holly tried to cradle the injured dog and comfort the little boy at the same time. In that instant she felt like she was in one of those movies in which you find yourself living someone else's life: a screaming child, an injured pet, a life-saving race to a veterinary hospital, motel-room thieves, an unknown sister, a mysterious past. This *couldn't* be her life. Any minute now she'd wake up and find herself asleep in her office, surrounded by letters waiting to be read.

"Good; someone's still here." Ben pulled up to the front door.

Ben lifted Dusty out of her arms. She looked down at her sweater, which was covered in blood. This couldn't be real.

"A little help," Ben called as a hysterical Bobby threatened to tear the unconscious dog from his arms.

Holly nodded her head and scrambled out of the car to open the door for Ben and restrain the sobbing child.

"Bring him right back," a man in a white coat instructed Ben.

"We'd better wait here." Holly grabbed Bobby's arm as he tried to follow. "We don't want to get in the way."

"But Dusty needs me," he sobbed.

"Ben will take care of him."

Holly maneuvered Bobby into one of the hard plastic chairs that lined one wall. She knelt down in front of the child and wrapped her arms around him as he sobbed. She couldn't remember ever having cried as hard as Bobby was crying in her entire life. The poor child's heart was breaking. First his parents, then his sisters; Holly was sure his little heart couldn't bear one more loss.

After what seemed like hours, Ben finally returned, covered with blood but with a smile on his face. "He's going to be fine. The doc assures me that with a little rest he'll be good as new."

"Can we take him home now?"

"Sorry, son. The doc wants to keep him overnight. He's given him a sedative, so he should be out for the night. We'll come back in the morning and check on him."

"Can I see him?"

Ben hesitated. Dusty must be hooked up to an IV and a heart monitor. Holly knew that the last thing he'd want to do was further scare the already hysterical little boy. On the other hand, he would know that Bobby wouldn't really believe that Dusty was okay if he didn't see so for himself.

"I'll check with the doctor."

Ben walked back through the doors he had just exited, only to return with the vet a few seconds later.

"Can I see my dog?" Bobby asked the doctor.

"I'll take you back, but you have to understand that we have him hooked up to some machines in order to help him get better faster. He's been sedated, so he won't know you're there, but I assure you he's going to be fine."

"Okay."

Ben and the doctor escorted Bobby back to the examining room, while Holly used the bathroom to wash some of the blood off her hands. As the blood washed into the white sink and down the drain, Holly felt herself begin to shake from delayed shock. Tears streamed down her face as she struggled to get her emotions under control before Ben and Bobby returned. Holly had just met Bobby, but she knew as she'd held him while he cried that she couldn't have hurt any more for him if he were her own child. She didn't know how parents managed to deal with the day-to-day traumas that inevitably touched their children's lives.

"He's sound asleep." Ben walked through the connecting doors into Holly's room a short time later.

"Poor thing. He's really had quite a day. I hope Dusty is going to be okay. Bobby seems really attached to him."

"The doctor assured me that he'd be fine. I'm not sure if we'll be able to continue our trip tomorrow as planned, though. The vet indicated he might want to keep him for a day or two."

"Bobby will be disappointed. He seemed excited about seeing his sisters tomorrow. Do you really think the grandmother will let him and his dog stay with her through the holidays?"

"God, I hope so." Ben sat down on the bed next to Holly. "I'm not sure what I'll do if she won't. I can't just turn him over to social services, especially this close to Christmas. He'll probably end up in a children's home. Maybe he can stay with my mother. If I can't convince the grandmother to let him stay with her, I'll call my mom and see if she'll take him in for a few weeks."

"Do you think social services will let him stay with your mom if it comes to that?"

"I don't know. I'm sure that particular scenario wouldn't fall into the parameters of normal protocol, but I still have some pull in high places. I think I could work it out."

"Meg would have taken them in. All of them, even Dusty." Holly felt a tear threaten in the corner of her eye. "I never stopped to consider what a really selfless and valuable thing she was doing all those years. I remember once, shortly after I had gone away to college, she took in this little boy around Bobby's age. He was a real terror. He'd been kicked out of seven foster homes. He was such a handful, and Meg was getting on in years. After he set fire to the barn, I tried to talk her into sending him away, but she wouldn't hear of it. She said that children weren't disposable and you didn't just get rid of them if they had a few problems. She loved him through all his anger and rebellion, and in the end she uncovered the beautiful person inside. It turns out that behind all the behavior problems was a brilliant mind. I saw him at Meg's funeral. He credits her with saving his life. If it hadn't been for Meg, he probably would have ended up in the criminal justice system on the wrong side of the bars."

"Meg was indeed an extraordinary person," Ben agreed, "She could see the beauty and potential in everyone she came into contact with. The world is a darker place without her."

"You really cared about her, didn't you?"

"Yeah, I did."

Ben sat quietly with Holly for several minutes before he leaned over and kissed her lightly on the lips. "I need to report the break-in to the police. I've checked around a little, and nothing seems to be missing, but the mess the intruders left behind indicates they were looking for something."

"Like what? What could any of us have with us that anyone would want?"

"I don't know. I won't be gone long. Lock the door behind me." Ben set his gun on the table next to the bed. "Do you know how to use one of these?"

"Sort of. I used to shoot tin cans with the guys after school."

"If anyone tries to break in, use it. Don't hesitate, just shoot. I'll be back as soon as I can."

"Ben . . ." Holly stopped him.

"Yeah?"

"Bobby said that Dusty getting hurt was his fault. Do you think there's something he's not telling us?"

"I doubt it, but maybe. We'll talk to him tomorrow. Now go and wash up. I'll be back as soon as I can."

Chapter 12

Saturday, December 7

"Holly." Bobby was pounding on the connecting door early the next morning. "Can I come in?"

"Sure. Come on in."

Bobby bonded into the room. Gone was the filthy hitchhiker with the chip on his shoulder, and in his place was an adorable little boy with blond curls, sparkling eyes, a huge grin, and boundless energy. "Ben and I are going to see Dusty. He wanted me to tell you that we'll get breakfast when we get back. He's over at the motel office, talking to the manager about the break-in."

"I'll get up and get showered right away so we can go to breakfast as soon as you get back. I hope Dusty's okay."

"Me, too. Maybe we can bring him home today. Ben said we'd have to see what the vet thought. We want to do what's right for him, even if we miss him."

"You're right, we do."

"See yah." Bobby bounded toward the door.

"Bobby . . ."

"Yeah?" He stopped and turned around.

"Last night you said that Dusty's getting hurt was your fault. What did you mean by that?"

Bobby paled. "Nothin'."

"Okay. I'll see you in a bit."

Holly watched him skip across the parking lot from the window. There was definitely something Bobby wasn't telling them, but what could a ten-year-old have that someone would break into a motel room to steal? Chances were Bobby was just feeling bad about taking Dusty along on the trip in the first place. Still, Holly knew a look of guilt when she saw one, and Bobby was definitely feeling bad about something.

After taking a shower and dressing, Holly decided to call Noel, who had returned her call the previous evening while they were at the movie theater. Noel had a tendency to worry about her, probably a byproduct of growing up with a revolving set of "siblings."

"Noel, it's Holly."

"Oh my God, Holly, where have you been? I've been frantic. I've left like ten messages."

"I'm so sorry." Holly felt guilty that she hadn't been better about checking her messages. "I didn't mean to worry you. I got an early Christmas present from Aunt Meg, and things have been a little crazy since then."

"Holly," Noel paused, concern in her voice, "Aunt Meg is dead. Are you okay? Do you need me to come? 'Cause I can be on the next plane."

"No, I'm not having a nervous breakdown. Aunt Meg arranged for my gift before she died."

"Really? What is it?"

"A man."

"A what?"

"Ben Holiday, to be exact."

"My Ben Holiday?"

"One and the same."

Noel was speechless. "Is there something I'm missing?"

"Quite a lot, actually. Have a seat and I'll explain everything."

Holly filled Noel in on the details of her adventure, glossing over the intensity of her developing feelings for Ben. It wasn't that she didn't want to share her feelings with her best friend; it was more that she really wasn't certain exactly what those feelings were. The guy was a total babe. It was natural to be attracted to him. Just because her heart beat a little faster whenever he was around and her palms tended to sweat when he held her hand certainly didn't mean she had *feelings* for him.

Holly realized that her entire emotional state could be chalked up to pheromones. It was best to stand back and retain a little distance. Besides, Ben didn't seem to be nearly as distracted by her as she was by him. Best to protect her heart before it got broken.

"You love him, don't you?" Noel asked.

"Huh?"

"Ben. You love him."

"I just told you that I might have found a sister I never knew I had and that my mother might be alive, and the only thing you can ask me is if I love Ben?"

"Well, do you?"

"Honestly?" Holly sighed. She never had been able to pull anything over on Noel. "I don't know. I'm attracted to him. He's sweet and considerate, and he has the sweetest smile I've ever seen. He's been really great with Bobby, and I feel happy when I'm with him. But love? How does one even know if what they're feeling is love?"

"You know."

Holly could hear the smile in Noel's voice.

"How about we change the subject for now?" Holly suggested. Maybe Noel was convinced that Holly was in love, but she sure as heck didn't want to discuss it with her before she even discussed it with Ben.

"Let's talk about the Winter Ball. Return to Sender is playing this year. You love that band. And Maggie Kline started a new catering business and is going to provide all the food. You know you can't resist Maggie's stuffed mushrooms," Noel said persuasively.

"I told you I wasn't sure I could get away," Holly reminded her.

"Please. I miss you so much. You can bring Ben. It'll be fun, I promise."

"Ben thinks you don't like him."

"What? Why not?"

"There was that little incident with Tommy at the bar . . ."

"Oh, that. Tommy told me what happened."

"In that case, I have to ask: you've tried to set me up with every breathing male in Moosehead. In two years' time, why haven't you tried to set me up with Ben?"

"Because you wouldn't have gone out with him. Every guy I set you up with you've hated on sight, no matter how great he was. I figured you'd find Ben in your own time. He's perfect for you, and Aunt Meg loved him like a son. You two will be very happy together."

"I never said we were getting married or, for that matter, had any other type of long-term future," Holly reminded her.

"You will. Aunt Meg said you would."

"Huh?"

"Aunt Meg and I had several heartfelt talks before she died. I told her I was worried about you, all alone in New York. She said she'd send you your one true love when you were ready. I had no idea who she was talking about at the time, but I guess she meant Ben."

"I swear, you and Aunt Meg are two peas in a pod." Holly couldn't help but chuckle. "Matchmakers to the end."

"Yeah, I really miss her. And I miss you. Please promise me you'll come home. If you don't want to go to the ball, we can skip it. Although," Noel hesitated, "I did buy a new dress. It's white. I know I usually go with red, but this dress is really spectacular. Please, please, please, come home for the dance."

Holly didn't want to let Noel down, but she wasn't sure what would happen with Ben after their journey was over, and she certainly didn't want to make any plans that included him in the meantime. She hoped that at the very least they'd remain friends, and he seemed to talk of their relationship in terms of the future, but to actually commit to something as romantic as the Winter Ball?

"I'll think about it," Holly replied. "I'm not sure where we'll be with this whole journey-into-the-past adventure, but if we've come to the end of our road and Ben is open to going to the ball, then maybe. I guess I should come home and figure out what to do with the house at the very least."

"Did you talk to Madison?"

"Yeah, she called a few days ago."

"And?"

"And she has an out-of-town buyer who wants to use the land to build a business park."

"A business park? What about the house?"

"He's planning to tear it down."

Noel was totally silent.

"Madison e-mailed the offer," Holly continued. "It's a good one. Enough so that I'd be able to afford to buy an apartment in the city."

"Are you going to do it?" Noel whispered, barely loud enough for Holly to hear her.

"I'm not sure. It makes sense from a business standpoint, but tearing down the house? There are a lot of memories in that house."

"Yeah, a lot of memories," Noel breathed.

Holly was certain Noel was crying, which made her feel a little more than awful. Noel loved Moosehead; she loved the house, and she loved the memories contained within its walls. There had been a time when Holly couldn't imagine not having the big white farmhouse to come home to. But now? Now things had changed.

"Ben and Bobby just pulled up," Holly informed her. "Don't worry about the house. I'm going to take some time to think about it, and I promise we'll talk about it before I do anything. I'll call you later."

"Doc said we could take Dusty home after he has a chance to check him out. He was awake and happy to see us. Wasn't he, Ben?" Bobby filled Holly in between bites of a giant stack of pancakes an hour later.

"He was, at that."

"He had this cone thing on his head so he couldn't scratch his stitches. He didn't seem to like it much, but the doc said it's important to let the wound heal."

"I'm sure he'll get used to it," Holly said.

"Ben said we should stay here another day so Dusty can rest before we continue with our trip. We should be able to get an early start tomorrow, though. If things go well, we should be in Phoenix in no time."

"I think that's a smart idea," Holly agreed. It was adorable how Bobby had taken to mimicking Ben word for word. She could see how a little boy who was all alone in the world would gravitate toward a man as strong and kind as Ben.

"I gotta go to the bathroom," Bobby announced.

"It's around the corner." Ben pointed the way.

"I asked Bobby what he meant about Dusty's injury being his fault, but he pretty much evaded the question," Holly informed Ben after Bobby had left.

"Yeah, I asked him about it, too. I'm going to take another look through his stuff when I get a chance. Maybe he took something from his uncle."

"Wouldn't the uncle just report it missing and let the police take care of it?"

"Not if Bobby took something illegal. His uncle was off gambling when Bobby took off. Gamblers have been known to participate in other questionable activities."

"Like drugs?" Holly guessed.

"Maybe. Or theft. Gambling habits can be expensive to support. Maybe Bobby took something with real or imagined value when he ran off. It wouldn't be hard for someone to follow us. I've stayed in contact with several agencies, including the social worker assigned to Bobby. I've given a description of our route and my vehicle to those who have asked. If Bobby's uncle was able to get that information, it would be easy to track us down if Bobby did take something he wanted back."

"So the uncle follows us, waits until we go out for the evening, and breaks in to retrieve his stolen goods. I guess at this point we're assuming the man didn't get what he was looking for, in which case we may still be in danger. I'll look through Bobby's stuff later while you take him to pick up Dusty," Holly offered.

"Sounds like a plan."

"What's a plan?" Bobby, who had just returned from the bathroom, asked.

"I thought we'd go swimming and then maybe have a picnic in the park, if Dusty's feeling better," Ben improvised.

A thorough search of Bobby's belongings uncovered nothing more valuable than the new pair of jeans Ben had bought him. Holly searched through all the pockets in both his new and old clothes, as well as the lining of his duffel bag. If Bobby had something, he'd hidden it well.

Holly neatly folded and replaced the clothes into the tattered bag just the way she'd found them, then returned the bag to the end of the bed where Bobby had left it and looked around, trying to see the room through different eyes. *If I were ten years old and wanted to hide something, where would I put it?*

Holly went into the bathroom, but the only thing Bobby had left behind was his worn toothbrush and a box of toothpaste. Holly thought it surprising that

Bobby had thought to bring such things when he ran away, but Bobby had informed her that his mom had always taught him about the importance of oral hygiene.

Holly walked out of the bathroom, then stopped and looked back. Odd that Bobby's toothpaste was still in the box. Returning to the bathroom, she opened the box and looked inside.

"Well, I'll be."

Chapter 13

Sunday, December 8

Bobby's grandmother lived in a two-story townhouse in an exclusive part of town. The black shutters displayed against white adobe gave the town home an elegant yet southwestern flare. Evergreen shrubs with bright red flowers lined the front walk. Bobby fidgeted nervously as Ben rang the bell and waited for someone to answer.

"Bobby, whatever are you doing here? And who are your friends?" the elderly woman, dressed in a shin-length brown dress, asked.

"My name is Ben Holiday and this is Holly," Ben said. "We'd like a few minutes of your time, if that's okay."

"Certainly. Come on in." The woman showed the trio to a parlor just off the entry. "Your sisters are in their room. Why don't you go and find them?" she directed Bobby.

Bobby let out the breath he had been holding and ran up the stairs, calling his sisters' names as he went.

"So much energy, that one. I tried to look after him, but his boyish enthusiasm and tendency to get into trouble was more than I could handle. The girls are calmer, better behaved, but Bobby can be a real handful. My health hasn't been good. I had to send him to stay with his uncle. Where is he, anyway?"

"Bobby ran away over a week ago. We found him trying to hitchhike toward Phoenix," Ben said, then filled her in on the details of their adventure.

"Oh my." The woman paled. She obviously cared about her grandson, in spite of her inability to take care of him. "I can't believe Toby didn't call and let me know what happened."

"He didn't know himself. He was away on a trip with some friends. He didn't even know Bobby was missing until I notified him."

"He left the child alone for a whole week?" The woman shook her head. "I don't know why I'm surprised; Toby never was a very responsible person. I just hoped he'd step up and take care of his sister's child. I guess that was expecting too much. I suppose I should call him and let him know that Bobby's okay."

"Actually, I believe he'll be unavailable for a while. It seems he got himself into a little bit of legal trouble," Ben said.

"Bobby was headed here, to see his sisters," Holly continued. "He really missed them."

"Yes, I imagine he did."

"I'd like to find a permanent placement for all three children so that they can be together," Ben explained. "With the holiday coming up, I doubt that will be possible until after the first of the year. I was hoping Bobby and his traveling companion could stay here until then."

"Traveling companion?"

"Dusty. His dog."

"I see. After everything that happened before, that seems like a lot to ask."

"I know," Ben admitted, "but I've had a talk with Bobby, and he's promised to be on his best behavior. I'll check in with you every day to see how things are going, and if there are any problems, I'll come and get him myself."

"And the dog? Has he promised to be on his best behavior as well?" the grandmother asked.

"Most definitely," Ben promised.

Holly smiled. The grandmother was going to go along with their plan; she could see it on her face. Now all they had to do was find a permanent placement for three kids and a dog. Piece of cake.

After Ben and Holly had been introduced to Bobby's sisters and they'd reiterated to Bobby that he had to be on his best behavior, they hugged him good-bye and got back into the Range Rover.

"I'm surprised you didn't fill the grandmother in on all the details of Uncle Toby's recent incarceration," Holly commented.

"I didn't want to bring up Bobby's part in the whole thing. I figured it was going to be hard enough to get her to agree to let him stay," Ben explained.

"It was pretty smart of him to hide the diamonds in plain sight. Most ten-year-olds wouldn't have the presence of mind to do so."

"Most ten-year-olds wouldn't have the presence of mind to take the stones in the first place."

"True. Why do you think he took them anyway?"

"I think his plan was to come to Phoenix, get his sisters, and strike out on their own."

"Do you think he'll be okay?" Holly couldn't help but be worried about the little boy who had wormed his way into her heart.

"Yeah, I think so. The police arrested the uncle and the man who broke into the motel room."

"And the diamonds?

"Returned to the dealer they were stolen from."

"Do you think there might be any more of his uncle's colleagues following Bobby?" Holly worried.

"I doubt it. I'm sure the word must have gotten out that the diamonds were recovered."

"Maybe we should stay in Phoenix tonight," Holly suggested as they pulled away from the two-story house. "Just in case."

"Just in case Bobby doesn't stick to his end of the bargain and his grandmother wants to send him packing, or just in case I'm wrong and Bobby really still is in danger?"

"Something like that," Holly said vaguely. "We could stay nearby and call in the morning to see how things are going. It doesn't feel right to just leave him here without knowing for sure whether things will work out."

"He got to you, didn't he?"

"Of course he got to me," Holly shot back. "He's ten years old and all alone in the world. You'd have to be subhuman not to care about what happens to him."

"Calm down. He got to me, too. Let's find a place to stay and then I'll take you out to dinner at this fantastic restaurant I found last time I was through this way. After dinner we'll call and check in with the grandmother."

The restaurant sat high on a hill overlooking the desert. Giant picture windows provided a 360-degree view of the area. Soft piano music played from overhead speakers and a crackling fire burned in a large pit in the center of the room.

A waiter showed them to a table near the window. A white linen tablecloth was adorned with forest-green linen napkins and a pine centerpiece ornamented with red and white roses.

"Wow, this place is beautiful." Holly stood beside the table and looked appreciatively around the room. "You can see the view in every direction. It's . . . wow."

"I thought you'd like it. And the best part is that the food is as good as the view."

"May I offer you a cocktail to start?" a formally dressed waiter asked.

"I'll have a vodka martini straight up," Holly said.

"Scotch on the rocks," Ben added.

"Our specials are listed on the back of the regular menu. I'll get your drinks, then be back to take your order and answer any questions."

"Everything looks so good." Holly studied the specials. "I think I'll try the duck. It sounds delicious. And I'll start with a house salad."

When the waiter returned, Ben ordered the duck for Holly and the lamb for himself, two house salads, and a bottle of wine to share.

"Do you come to Phoenix often?" Holly asked as she stared out of the window.

"Not as often as I'd like. I bring my bike sometimes. There's something about taking off across the open desert, the wind at your back. Nothing compares to the freedom you feel when you're flying across the landscape. It's a totally liberating experience. How about you? What sets your soul free?"

Holly smiled wickedly.

"Besides that." Ben laughed.

"At the moment, I can't think of another thing. I noticed a dance floor at the back of the room when we came in. Care to work up an appetite?"

Ben cleared his throat. "Uh, sure."

The dance floor was empty except for one other couple who seemed completely lost to the world around them. Holly molded her body to Ben's as they began to sway to the piano music. The corner of the room was dark except for the small white lights that decorated the Christmas tree. Holly could feel her heartbeat quicken as she relaxed in Ben's arms. It felt so right. So natural to have his arms around her.

Time seemed to stand still as they swayed to the music. Holly felt Ben's breath on her neck as he held her close. She didn't think she was interested in a relationship at this point in her life, but in that moment she realized that she could stay, right here in this room, swaying to the music, forever.

Ben took a deep breath and a half step back. "I think they brought our salads. Maybe we should . . ."

"Huh. Oh, sure. Let's eat." Holly unwound her arms from around Ben's neck and looked around the room, as if trying to remember where they were.

"This way." Ben placed his palm on the small of her back and led her to their table.

Ben was trying to appear unaffected by their dance, but Holly could see the passion in his eyes. Maybe all they'd ever have were these brief moments between them. Maybe they'd finish their journey and return to their separate lives. But then again . . .

Chapter 14

Monday, December 9

Ben and Holly both slept late the next morning. By the time they called Bobby's grandmother to confirm that things were indeed going well and had a meal, it was after noon before they got on the road.

Holly had talked to Phillip, who was continuing to pressure her into returning to New York sooner rather than later. She figured they would pull into Houston tomorrow afternoon; she could spend the following day with her sister, if Sarah was so inclined, and she could fly home on Thursday. She really wanted to follow the journey to the end and even if she talked to Sarah she might not have all her answers, but Phillip was certain that if she put the meeting off much longer she'd lose the opportunity altogether.

The landscape between Phoenix and Houston was both barren and beautiful in Holly's opinion. Dark clouds were rolling in from the south, and the National Weather Service had issued a strong storm warning for later that afternoon.

If there was one thing that could be said for the wide-open desert, it was that you could see for miles in every direction. "Looks like the storm they're talking about on the news is making its way in this direction," Holly stated the obvious.

"Yeah. Sounds like it could get intense. Even if we don't have to stop early due to the storm, we won't get to Houston until fairly late tomorrow afternoon, so I suggest we get a room near the campus, then look Sarah up on Wednesday. Might be a good idea to call ahead for a reservation."

"I'll do that as soon as we get to an area that has service." Holly held up her phone to reveal no lines. "Once we get to the campus, how are we going to find her?"

"I'm working on getting the location of her classes. We'll get a campus map when we get there. It shouldn't be too hard to track her down."

"I'm really nervous." Holly kicked off her shoes, then folded her legs up under her. "I mean, like heart-pounding, ready-to-jump-out-of-my-skin nervous."

Ben wound the fingers of his right hand through the fingers of her left. "I understand your nervousness, but it'll be fine. I'll be right there with you the whole time."

"What if she hates me?"

"She won't."

"What if she resents my interference in her life?"

"She won't."

"What if we have nothing in common and our meeting is awkward and uncomfortable?"

"Then we'll promise to keep in touch and make an excuse to make a quick exit. Keep in mind that speaking to your sister may not answer all your questions anyway."

Holly sat quietly as the road turned sharply toward the south and the approaching storm. In a way, she felt like that storm, slowly brewing and building in intensity until it finally burst onto the surrounding landscape. Holly couldn't ever remember having so much nervous energy and no way to burn it off.

"Finding out I have a sister was so weird."

"I know."

"According to the waitress at the café, she looks exactly like me."

"I know."

"Wouldn't it be strange to find out there was someone in the world who looked exactly like you?"

"It would."

"Oh God. She's going to hate me. I think I'm going to be sick."

Ben slowed the car a bit and turned to face her. "Just breathe. Slow breath in, slow breath out."

Holly followed his instructions.

"Don't you feel better?"

"No."

"Do you want me to stop?" Ben asked.

"No, I'll be okay. I just need a distraction."

"So how hot was that dance last night?"

Holly smiled. "Good distraction."

"Maybe we should play one of those car games."

"Car games?"

"Yeah, you know, like trying to find a license plate from every state."

"We haven't seen another car in twenty minutes," Holly pointed out.

"When I was a kid, we played this game where you had to find something that started with each letter of the alphabet, and whoever got through the whole alphabet first won."

"Other than dirt, sagebrush, pavement, and clouds, I'd say we're going to have a hard time with that one, too. How about Twenty Questions?"

"Sounds perfect," Ben agreed. "You go first."

By the time Ben was on question eight, it had started to rain. By question eleven, hail. And when he rounded the corner of question fifteen, the visibility around them faded to the point at which he decided to pull over to the side of the road.

"Wow. I've never seen a storm quite like this one." Holly looked out of the window nervously. "I've been seeing flash-flood warning signs for several miles. Do you think we're in any danger?"

"I'm not sure." Ben frowned. "It doesn't feel like we're in a low spot, but it's hard to see much of anything. There's no way we can continue until it lets up a bit, so we have no choice but to stay put. Storms don't usually get quite so intense this time of year."

Holly turned on the radio and found a station listing counties that had been issued tornado warnings. "Any idea what county we're in?"

"No idea," Ben answered. He tried to pull up the GPS on his phone but was unsuccessful. "I have paper maps in the back, but I'm not really thrilled about getting out to go back to get them."

"I'll get them." Holly unbuckled her seat belt and climbed over the seat. "Are we in Texas or Arizona still?"

"Actually, I think we've passed into New Mexico," Ben said.

Holly grabbed both the New Mexico and Texas maps, and they worked together to try to determine their approximate location, then listened to the storm warnings again. The announcer on the radio announced there were a series of strong cells in the area and listeners should take cover immediately.

"I've run into storms like this in my travels and they usually pass pretty quickly," Ben said, trying to comfort her. "There was this one time I was driving out across the flatlands of South Dakota and got caught in this extremely intense storm. Huge bolts of lightning hit the ground all around me for miles in every direction. I remember wondering about the cows that continued to graze the grasslands while the electrical event was lighting up the early evening sky."

"Did any of them get hit?" Holly wondered.

"I didn't notice any dead cows lying about, but common sense would tell you that sometimes the cows must fall victim to the weather."

"Like those cows flying through the air in the movie *Twister*," Holly reminded him.

"Yeah. I mean, there are tornadoes out across those flatlands all the time. I wonder if that really happens? It might be kind of cool to see a tornado up close. I was almost in one about four years ago. I was traveling through Oklahoma, and there was a really intense storm like this one, so I pulled over to wait it out. After the rain let up a bit, I continued west, the direction I was heading at the time, and found out that an F4 had blown across the road just five miles away from where I sat waiting."

"Wonderful," Holly groaned.

"Guess that wasn't the best story to tell at this particular time," Ben realized.

"I will say that we've certainly had the full range of weather on this trip. The blizzard in the north, the heat in Phoenix, and now this."

"With Ben Holiday, you get the complete travel experience," Ben said, sounding like a commercial for a travel agency.

"Shh, there's an update." Holly turned up the sound on the radio as the announcer informed them that there had been several tornadoes spotted in the area.

"See what you've done," Holly complained.

"What *I've* done?"

"You're the one who wanted to see a tornado. If we get swirled up into one, it'll be your fault." Holly looked at the map and used her pen to circle the towns that had been mentioned. "Looks like we're right in the middle of it."

Ben frowned. "We should try to get off this open road. The problem is that the next town is quite a ways away, and in this rain we'll only be able to drive about five miles an hour."

"The hail has turned to rain and it looks like it's letting up a bit," Holly offered. "Maybe we should go for it."

"Yeah, maybe, but we really have no way of knowing if the storm is better or worse in front of us. If I had reception on my phone, I could pull up the National Weather Service and get a view of the Doppler."

Holly looked out the window. The landscape was becoming clearer as the intensity of the rain decreased.

"There's a town over here." Ben pointed to a town on the map, just down the road and to the right. "I'm guessing it's at the foothills of that little mountain range over there." He pointed into the distance. "It's probably nothing more than a hole in the wall, but it's a lot closer than the next town on this road."

Holly hesitated. Ben had a point about the rain letting up a bit, but she didn't like the look of the clouds either behind or in front of them. It almost appeared that the storm was worse in both directions than it was where they were standing. "We might be able to find a safer place to wait out the rain."

"It might not be a good idea to venture off the main road when we really don't know what we're getting into," Ben warned. "Let's give it a few more minutes. We'll wait for the next weather update and see if the tornado warnings are moving toward or away from us. Besides, the rainwater seems to be running away from us. If we head out, there's no assurance that we won't hit a low spot and run into a flash-flood situation."

Holly hated waiting, but Ben was right. For the moment, they didn't seem to be in any imminent danger. She adjusted the dial on the radio to see if there were other stations that might have additional or different information. Most stations were playing music and not even referring to the weather, so Holly turned back to the station they had been listening to.

"It's so odd not to have cell service," Holly commented. "I keep thinking that I'll use this down time to return phone calls, and then I remember I have no service. Yet a minute later the same thought flutters through my mind."

"I know what you mean. When I lived in New York, I automatically reached for my cell dozens of times a day. The cell service at the lake where I live now is pretty lousy, so I've become less dependent on it. Still, it would be good to get a bird's-eye view of what we're sitting in the middle of."

There was a loud bang as thunder rumbled through the area.

"Did you see lightning?" Holly asked.

"No, you?"

Holly shook her head. "This is really freaking me out. Let's take our chances on the road."

"You're the boss." Ben turned on the ignition and slowly eased onto the highway. They headed slowly down the road as the storm lessened but the clouds darkened.

"Over to your left," he said, directing Holly's attention to dark clouds from which he'd just seen a flash of light a second before another loud crash. "I don't think the lightning is hitting the ground. It seems to be contained within the cloud."

"Is that a good thing?" Holly wondered.

"I have to confess I'm really not sure, although it seems like lightning in the sky is better than lightning hitting the ground. This road is taking us away from that particular cloud, so maybe you were right to suggest we head on down the road. Keep an eye out for any service lines. If I can pull up the National Weather Service on my phone, we'll have a better idea of what we're heading into. Hopefully it's not one of those out-of-the-frying-pan-into-the-fire scenarios."

Holly monitored both the radio and the cell phone coverage while Ben slowly drove toward an increasingly darkening sky. The landscape around them was completely flat, making Holly feel like a target on the empty road. Was staying in your car a good choice or not? Holly wished she hadn't changed the channel every time one of the news anchors gave severe-weather tips and advice.

"What's that over there?" Holly pointed to a narrow road to the right that looked like it hadn't been maintained in years.

"Must be the little town on the map. Think we should check it out?"

Holly jumped as thunder echoed through the countryside. "Yeah, let's take a look. I don't like those clouds in front of us. Is the town very far off the road?"

"The map makes it seem like it's maybe ten miles away at the foot of that mountain range. If nothing else, the mountains might provide some protection from the storm. Maybe we'll be able to get to a television to get a weather update. And at the very least, we should be able to find a phone."

Holly jumped when the cloud with the lightning grew closer. "Let's give it a try."

Ben drove slowly along the heavily rutted road, watching for low points and standing water as they went. The sight of old stone buildings standing alone at the base of a small mountain was about as eerie as Holly had ever seen. Flashbacks to every horror film she'd ever watched had her rethinking the sanity of taking refuge in one of the abandoned structures.

"It looks like it's nothing more than a ghost town," Ben said, slowing the car.

"Ghost town?"

"I don't think there are actual ghosts," Ben teased. "Mostly just old and decaying buildings abandoned by the mining company that used to work the area. There are a lot of towns like this in the desert. This one looks like it's been deserted for quite some time."

"This is so *Twilight Zone*," Holly whispered as Ben pulled up in front of the building that looked to be in the best state of repair and turned off the car. "We're all alone in the middle of nowhere, in an abandoned town, in the middle of a storm with tornadoes all around us, no cell service, and no way to contact anyone or get back to the road if anything were to happen to the car."

"Sounds about right." Ben was looking around, but he didn't make a move to get out of the car. "What do you want to do?"

"I'm not sure." The last thing Holly wanted was to spend time in this eerie little town, and every instinct she possessed urged her to flee back to the highway, but as a thundercloud moved directly overhead, she began to think they would be wise to take their chances with the ghosts. A crumbling building seemed like a better choice than no building at all. "I guess we should find some cover until the worst of the storm passes."

"It looks like there's the mouth of a mine shaft just up that hill." Ben pointed into the distance. "Probably a good choice, at this point."

"Mine shaft?" Holly hated the idea.

"It's underground, so even if a tornado hits, we should be fine."

"Underground?"

"Don't worry. We'll wait near the entrance. I have flashlights, so we won't have to wait in the dark. We're going to have to make a run for it. Ready?"

"Not even a tiny little bit." Holly opened her door and counted to three as Ben opened his and they ran toward the shaft opening together.

There was a short tunnel leading to a ladder that led down into the earth. "We're not going down there, are we?" Holly shivered, more from fear than the cold.

"No, we'll wait it out here. We should be perfectly safe with the mountain overhead."

"Unless there's a cave-in," Holly said.

"There won't be a cave-in. Let's just wait near the entrance and watch for the storm to pass, and then we'll head back to the car."

Ben found a relatively flat place to sit and leaned back against the wall of the shaft, pulling Holly down between his legs. He wrapped his arms around her and eased her back against his chest. "Better?"

Holly leaned her head against his chest and listened to his heart beat. She suddenly felt a lot better. The rain outside the shaft was coming down in sheets, but in Ben's arms she felt safe and warm. She closed her eyes and let herself pretend they were somewhere other than an abandoned mine, on the outskirts of a ghost town.

Ben stroked her hair and began to talk to her in a slow, soothing voice. He told her of his travels and some of the interesting things he'd seen on the road. He talked about all of the places he wanted to take her, all of the things he wanted to show her. He rubbed her arms and her back and described in detail the hysterical antics of an old Southern black man who'd been his guide on one of his cases, involving a missing heiress in the bayous of Louisiana.

As he spoke, the rain stopped and the wind stalled. Holly was almost asleep by the time Ben suggested they venture outside to take a look. She didn't want to leave what had become a cozy cocoon, but it would be getting dark soon, so she knew it was best to get on their way. Standing at the entrance to the mine shaft, they looked out over the town from the elevated height.

"It's so strange to think that this was once a bustling mining town, with people who lived out their lives here." Ben tucked his arm around her waist as they surveyed the landscape. "I can almost picture residents walking in the streets, having a drink at the saloon, or sharing a Sunday morning service in the chapel up on the hill."

Holly looked up the little hill at the chapel, one of the few wooden buildings in the little town, which had been built mostly of stone. "Why all the stone?" Holly wondered.

"Look around; no trees. Guess they used what materials they had available at the time they built the town. The stone has held up better than wood would have. Quite a few of these structures look pretty solid. Wanna take a look around?"

"Maybe we should just head back to the car," Holly said. The term *ghost town* was echoing through her mind again. Not that she believed in ghosts—at least not to the point where she was really afraid of running into one. Still, the rain seemed to have let up, and they had a few hours of light left. "We should check the radio for an update. If the storm has passed, we can find a motel in the next town and continue on to Houston tomorrow."

"Everything is so quiet." Ben stepped outside. The rain had completely stopped and the air was still.

Holly and Ben walked hand in hand back to the Range Rover. She opened the passenger door, leaned inside, and turned on the radio. "Shh," she directed, as she turned up the radio and tried to make out what the announcer was saying over the static. "Oh my God," she whispered. "Did you hear that?"

The radio announcer somberly informed the listening audience that a series of tornadoes had hit several towns in the area, including the one they'd talked about heading toward, destroying buildings and injuring residents in the process. So far, no fatalities had been reported, but the highway on which they had been traveling had been closed in both directions so the authorities could assess the damage and clean up the debris. It was predicted that the road would be closed for a minimum of twelve hours.

"It'll be okay," Ben said, trying to comfort her. "I'm sure they'll have it cleared up by morning. We have shelter and blankets. We'll wait here."

"With the ghosts?" Holly paled.

Chapter 15

Tuesday, December 10

Tuesday morning dawned bright and sunny. The sky was bluer than Holly had ever remembered seeing it. The rain had left behind a feeling of rebirth and renewal as desert creatures emerged from their dens to enjoy the warm sun. Holly tried to work the crick out of her neck as she quietly untangled herself from Ben's arms, where she'd fitfully passed the night, and crawled out of the vehicle.

It hadn't been as bad as it could have been. The backseat of the SUV folded down to form an uncomfortable but adequate sleeping area. Ben had a stash of blankets in his emergency supplies, and they'd even found an apple, a banana, and half a bag of chips left over from their travels with Bobby.

After assessing their situation, Ben had gathered some dry wood and built a fire. They'd cuddled under the blankets and pondered the night sky. The stars in Minnesota were fantastic, but Holly doubted she'd ever seen quite the number she'd witnessed under the desert sky.

The evening had been beautiful but nerve-racking. The old stone buildings rose up like dim shadows against the stark backdrop of the night as fragments of whispered memories lingered in the background. With each unexplained noise, Holly found her apprehension growing as total silence mingled with the echo of long-ago conversations just beyond her hearing.

It helped that Ben had been there. He'd been so thoughtful and attentive as he tried to anticipate her every need. He'd walked with her into the darkness so that she could attend to nature's call, turning his back but talking to her all the while, so she wouldn't feel completely alone with the spirits of the town's residents lingering in the darkness. He told her stories of his youth, which, like those of his travels, were funny and endearing. Several of the stories were so ridiculous she was certain he had made them up, but between the fire, which he continued to feed, and the carefree lilt of his voice, she found herself distracted from their isolation.

After a while, when Holly's eyes finally began to droop, he'd bundled her up and settled her into his arms in the back of the Range Rover, where he'd held her tightly through the night. If she didn't love him before, she knew she did now. She didn't know what that meant for them. Maybe nothing. A harsh truth, the fact remained that love wasn't always enough.

What she did know was that she was never going to make it back to New York by Friday. Phillip would have a cow, but the reality was that the storm had set them back a day, and there was no way she was going to abandon her journey when she was so close. Phillip seemed certain that putting the meeting off was going to jeopardize the whole thing, but the more Holly thought about it, the less certain she was that he was being completely honest with her. Who negotiated those types of deals a few weeks before Christmas? Chances were that Phillip was just being Phillip.

Holly smiled as a cottontail bunny scurried into one of the buildings as she headed into the ruins of the town. In the bright light of day, the old stone structures didn't seem nearly as spooky as they had during the storm and under the night sky. Still, she hoped the road was open; the rumble in her stomach reminded her that she hadn't had much to eat the night before.

Holly peeked into one of the buildings and noticed an old mattress and some dishes. Another structure looked as if it had once been a bar, while yet another contained the machinery they'd most likely used to mine whatever it was they'd mined all those years ago. She climbed an overgrown path to the little church on the hill. The graveyard was overgrown with wild grasses after years of being left unattended. Walking among the decaying headstones made Holly sad in a melancholy sort of way.

Real people had once lived in the town. They'd loved here, and married here, and born children, and lived out their lives. She wondered what had happened to the little town. How and when had it died? Was it a slow death, with people moving away over time until eventually everyone had gone? Or had it been a more abrupt departure due to disease or a specific cataclysmic event? Perhaps the mine had dried up and everyone had simply moved on.

It saddened Holly that the memories of those buried in the little cemetery were destined to be left behind. She wondered if anyone ever thought of Jolene Campbell, a thirty-two-year-old wife and mother who died in 1917, or Jeremiah Smith, the forty-seven-year-old father who died a year later? Holly pulled the dead grass away from a small grave with a headstone that simply read BABY BOY TURNER.

"I love old cemeteries." Ben walked up behind her and wrapped his arms around her waist. "It's sobering to remember that so many people have walked this earth before us. People just like us, with hopes and dreams and jobs and families."

"It's sad that it's been abandoned."

"You know that old cemetery at the end of Donaldson Road just outside of Moosehead?"

"Yeah. The gravestones in it are over a hundred years old."

"The past two springs, I rode my bike up there and cleaned it up a bit. Pulled the weeds, repaired the stones, planted a few bright flowers."

"Really?" Holly turned so that they were facing each other. Ben tightened his grip around her and she wrapped her arms around his neck. "Why?"

"I'm not sure. The first year I moved to Beaver Lake, after Peg's death, I was feeling really lost and went for a ride. I came across the old cemetery and it hit me how fragile life really is. I got off my bike and walked around the cemetery, crying like a baby the whole time. I knelt down and pulled away the weeds from a gravesite in order to get a better look at it. After that I just sort of continued to pull weeds as I went, reading about each person and wondering about their life. I found it oddly cathartic. After I cleared out all the weeds and garbage, I bought some yellow and red flowers and planted them around. The project took several weeks, but by the time I had finished, I realized I had, on some level, come to grips with Peg's death. I went back last year and plan to do so again this year, and every year I live there."

"That's a beautiful story." Holly felt tears threatening.

"Sometimes the universe shows us a way to deal with our grief. For me, it was an old cemetery; for you, it might be something entirely different."

"You don't think I've dealt with my grief?" Holly asked.

"Have you?"

Holly didn't answer. She knew Ben was right. She liked to think that she had moved on after Meg's death, but deep in her heart she knew she hadn't. She liked Ben's story about the graveyard. Maybe she needed to find her own graveyard, either literally or figuratively. After she found her sister and figured out the mystery of her past. Then she'd need to find a way to move on.

Ben placed his hand on the side of her face, wiping away the single tear that trailed down her cheek with his thumb. "I love you," he whispered. "I don't know if that means anything for us, but I wanted you to know."

Holly started to say something, but Ben placed a finger over her lips. "Later. Whatever you were going to say, you can say it later. For now, let's find your sister and put this mystery to rest."

Chapter 16

Wednesday, December 11

Wednesday morning dawned bright and sunny. After returning to the highway, the trip the previous day had been long but uneventful. Ben's contact had called back with Sarah's class schedule, so the only thing left to do was to make the short trek to the campus.

"Are you ready?" Ben asked as he picked Holly up at the door to her room.

"I guess. How do I look? Do I look okay? Maybe we should have gone shopping for new clothes. This blouse is totally old. I threw this outfit into my suitcase at the last minute."

"You look beautiful." Ben told her that he loved the freewheeling jeans-clad woman he'd been traveling with these past weeks, but he couldn't help but appreciate the slightly more sophisticated Holly who met him at the door dressed in light gray slacks, a pink and gray sleeveless blouse, and three-inch stiletto heels. Her long blond hair hung loosely down her back, and she'd taken care that her makeup was just right.

"Really?"

"Absolutely."

"Okay, let's do this."

Holly walked hand in hand with Ben out of the motel and into the parking lot. She couldn't believe how nervous she was. She realized nerves were to be expected, but she hadn't realized quite how terrified she'd really feel. She wanted to do this, she really did. But with each step she took toward the waiting SUV, she had to forcefully prevent herself from fleeing back to the safety of her room.

After obtaining a campus map, Ben and Holly parked in visitor parking and set off to find Holly's other half. They'd consulted her schedule and determined that Sarah would be between classes They decided to try the cafeteria closest to the physics department.

"Oh God, there she is," Holly whispered as they stood just inside the door.

Sarah was standing in line, tray in hand, talking to a girl behind her. Except for the fact that she had shorter hair, she looked exactly like Holly.

"What do I say?" Holly asked.

"I'm not sure."

"Big help you are. Maybe we should leave and figure out how we're going to spring this on her. We can come back later. Besides, I think I'm going to throw up. I can't believe how scared I am. She's going to hate me."

"She won't hate you, and I think we should do it now," Ben argued. "From what I can tell, Sarah's finished with classes for the day. That'll give us time to talk."

"What if she doesn't want to talk?"

"She will."

"I really think . . ." Holly's argument was interrupted by a loud crash.

Sarah stood staring at them, a stunned expression on her face, her lunch displayed haphazardly at her feet. Holly hesitated for just a second, then grabbed Ben's hand and hurried forward. "I'm Holly. I'm your sister," she blurted out.

"My what?"

"I'm your twin sister." Tears streamed down Holly's face. "I'm sorry. I should have handled this better. I know it's a lot to take in."

Sarah looked like she might pass out. "I have a sister?"

"Is there somewhere we can talk?" Ben took control of the situation. "Somewhere private?"

Sarah looked down at the mess at her feet.

"It's okay; I'll get it," the girl who was with her offered.

Sarah lifted her head and looked at Holly. Then she looked around the cafeteria, as if she were trying to figure out what it was she was supposed to do. "My roommate's out," she whispered. "We can go to my apartment."

Ben and Holly followed Sarah back to her apartment. No one said a word as they walked.

"Have a seat," Sarah offered.

Holly sat on the sofa and Ben sat on a desk chair, while Sarah just stood in the middle of the living room and stared at them both.

"How could this happen?" Sarah finally asked.

Holly looked to Ben, tears coursing down her cheeks, begging him with her eyes to explain the whole story. She wanted to explain, to say something, anything, that would offer comfort to her sister, but she couldn't speak.

"Holly didn't find out about the possibility that she had a sister until two weeks ago, when she received a rather unexpected Christmas present." Ben went over the entire story from start to finish, injecting just the right amount of humor to keep things light and comfortable. He explained about the necklaces and the two car seats. He talked about

Meg's desire for him to help Holly find her identity. He told her about following the clues from John Remington to Lilly Walton and finally to Marge at the diner.

"Poor Marge." Sarah laughed. "She must have thought she was seeing a ghost. I'm betting the whole town knows about my look-alike by now."

"She was a little shocked at first, but not half as much as we were." Holly chuckled, finally beginning to relax. Things were going to be okay. Sarah was smiling and the color had returned to her face.

"What I don't understand is why I was with my mom and you were with her sister," Sarah said. "I've always known I was adopted, but my mom sort of glossed over the circumstances of my birth. She told me that I was born to a friend of hers who couldn't keep me and swore her to secrecy. That really doesn't explain why she never told me about you."

"That's a question we'd like to have answered, too," Holly confirmed.

"I'll call her." Sarah started toward the phone. She had just picked up the receiver when there was a knock at the door. Setting the receiver back in its cradle, she opened the door. "Mom?"

Rosa froze when she saw Holly sitting behind Sarah.

"My baby, I'm so, so sorry," Rosa cried. She stepped into the room and folded Sarah in her arms. "I came as soon as I heard. I hoped to get to you first, so that I could explain."

"Explain?" Sarah asked. "How could you have known I had a sister and not told me?"

"I thought she was dead," Rosa sobbed. "I thought they all were."

"Maybe you should start at the beginning," Ben suggested. He led Rosa over to the dining table in the center of the room.

Rosa sat down on the chair Ben had pulled out for her. Sarah sat down next to her. Holly hesitated but stayed where she was on the sofa. Ben handed Rosa a box of tissue he'd found in the bathroom. Everyone waited while Rosa struggled to control her emotions. Finally she began to speak.

"Until this morning, I thought your sister was dead," she began. "My sister Monica used to work sometimes for a man who lived in Gardiner by the name of Carl Langley." Tears continued to course down her face as she struggled with her story. "One day she went with her husband, Nehemiah, to bring the man some groceries. When they got to Mr. Langley's house, he was dead on the floor and your biological mother was deep into labor. Monica claimed that she helped deliver the babies, but the poor mother had lost a lot of blood and was very weak and barely conscious. It looked likely that she would not survive. Monica wanted to take the woman to the hospital, but she refused to go. She said that a man named Smitty was after her. He intended to kill all three of them. She was too weak to protect you, so she asked Monica to take you away in her car while she led them in the opposite direction. Nehemiah and Monica drove an old truck with a single bench seat, so they decided to take Carl's old station wagon. They went in one direction and the woman who had given birth to you went in another."

"So how did Holly and Sarah become separated?" Ben asked.

"Monica and Nehemiah stopped at my house on their way out of town. I'm not proud to admit this, but I was jealous that Monica had two babies and I had none. I offered to carry Sarah back to the car when they were ready to leave, but when they got to the car, I told Monica that if she didn't leave Sarah behind, I'd call the authorities and report the whole thing. Monica tried to argue with me, but after I agreed to take good care of the baby and to give her back to the mother if she ever showed up, she finally left."

"That explains the two car seats and the two diaper bags in the car I was found in," Holly replied. "But why didn't you ever report that your sister was missing?"

"I didn't want the authorities to find out about Sarah. They would have taken her and put her in a foster home."

"Which is where I ended up," Holly pointed out. "No one ever knew who I was or where I had come from."

"I didn't know that," Rosa said, defending herself. "When I saw on the news that the car Monica had been riding in was in an accident and the occupants of the car were burned beyond recognition, I figured you were all dead. I didn't see how notifying the authorities of Monica's disappearance could help. I was trying to protect my baby. I didn't want them to take her away."

Sarah had yet to say anything, but she was staring at her mom like she was an alien from another planet. "You didn't see how it could help?" she finally spat out. "If you had reported this whole thing to the authorities, chances are they would have realized who

Holly was. We might have grown up together in the same house as sisters."

"I'm sorry." Rosa started sobbing again. "I handled it poorly. I just wanted you so much."

"I don't know if I can forgive you." Sarah dropped her head and looked down at her hands, which were folded in her lap.

Holly got up from the sofa and sat down next to Sarah. She'd just met the woman, but she understood what it meant to find the part of yourself that instinctively she'd always known was missing. "I know this is a lot to take in, but I can see that your mom loves you very much. I will admit that she could have handled things better, but I know what it is to want something so very, very badly that you'll do anything to get it."

Sarah looked up at Holly.

"I grew up with a wonderful woman who I know loved me as much as any mother can love a daughter," Holly said. "Still, like you, I felt angry and betrayed when I first discovered that she knew things about my past she'd never told me. I didn't understand how she could say that she loved me, yet keep such a huge secret from me."

"Do you understand now?" Sarah asked.

Holly shrugged. "Not really. But I do know that since Meg died, I've missed her more than I thought I could miss anyone. If I had the chance to have her back in my life, even if it meant never finding out what I have now, I'd take that chance in a minute."

Sarah looked at Rosa, who continued to sob. "Do you know what happened to my mother?" she asked.

"No. I swear to you. I never heard another word about the woman who gave birth to you that day.

Monica said your mother drove in the opposite direction so she could escape with you, but I swear she never came looking for you."

"Okay," Sarah said.

"Okay?" Rosa smiled.

"Yeah. We're good."

Mother and daughter cried as they embraced.

"But I want some time with my sister." Sarah pulled away after a few minutes. "Go home. I'll be there in a few days, as planned."

"I'll drive you to the airport," Ben offered.

"Did she get a flight okay?" Holly asked two hours later, when Ben walked back in with a bagful of food.

"Yes. Luckily, they had one that was about to board. She managed to breeze thorough security, since she didn't have luggage. She must have headed straight for the airport and caught the first flight she could get after Marge told her that she'd seen Sarah's look-alike."

"She must have realized who you were," Sarah said.

"What'd you bring?" Holly asked.

"Chinese." Ben set the bag on the dining table. "I figured we never got a chance to eat, and Sarah dropped her lunch."

"Wow, that's quite some guy you have there," Sarah commented to Holly.

"Yeah, he really is." Holly gazed at the man who had taken on an impossible task and had totally come through. He'd given her a sister, and for that she would forever be in his debt.

While they ate, Ben kept the conversation light in order to give everyone an emotional break. As Holly listened to him liberally embellish story after story in the spirit of humor, she realized that half of the things he'd told her the night of the storm had probably been fiction. Still, it was so sweet, the way he was totally putting himself out there so that everyone would feel comfortable.

"I'm teaching a class in an hour," Sarah informed them after they had finished their meal. "I should be done around six; maybe we could have dinner?"

"We'd love to." Holly stood up and hugged her newly discovered sister. "We'll pick you up here at say six thirty?"

"That'd be perfect."

"I think that went well," Ben commented as he walked hand in hand with Holly back to the car.

"Better than well. I really like her. And not just because she shares my blood. She's funny and smart and caring."

"Yeah, she's really great. And pretty too," Ben teased.

"Now don't you go falling for her," Holly flirted.

"Don't worry. My heart's already taken."

Holly smiled and twirled around in a circle. "I feel good. Really good. I haven't felt this good in a long, long time." Holly hugged Ben and kissed him hard on the lips. "Don't you feel good?"

"I'm starting to."

"I'm not talking about that kind of good." Holly playfully punched his arm.

"I know," Ben said, rubbing his arm and feigning injury. "I do feel good. It makes me feel good to see you so happy."

"Let's go shopping," Holly suggested.

"Shopping?"

"I've been wearing the same few clothes for over a week. I want to get something new. Something fun."

"Okay. Shopping it is."

Holly bought a new pair of slacks that hugged her frame and a soft cashmere sweater, and a sexy dress for dinner and a pair of strappy sandals to go with it. And finally, after sending Ben off in search of coffee, she bought the sexiest teddy she could find. She might not need it quite yet, but one day soon . . . Afterward, they headed back to the motel to shower and dress for dinner.

"You'd better grab a coat," Ben suggested when he picked Holly up at her door.

"The only coat I brought was my down jacket, and it so won't go with this dress."

Ben shrugged out of his suit jacket. "Well, at least wear this until we get to the restaurant."

Holly wrapped the jacket around her. It was still warm from his body and smelled like him, musky. Not as good as the real thing, but definitely enough to send her thoughts along a path not really appropriate for a night out with her sister.

They knocked on Sarah's apartment door at exactly six thirty. A tall brunette answered on the second knock.

"Wow. You really do look like her. I'm Marcy, Sarah's roommate. She went to the student lounge to meet Jeremy, so she asked me to take you there."

"Jeremy?" Holly asked.

"Sarah's fiancé. She wanted you to meet him."

"Sarah's engaged?"

"Yeah. He's really nice; you'll like him. He's totally going to flip when he sees you. But don't let him talk you into going along with any of his experiments. He's doing a doctorate in psychology and always wants to try stuff out on everyone. Twin sisters who were separated at birth and meet for the first time twenty-seven years later; he'd have a field day."

"Thanks. I'll keep that in mind."

"Holly!" Sarah ran up and hugged her as soon as they walked into the lounge. "This is my fiancé, Jeremy. Jeremy, Holly," she introduced.

"Wow." Jeremy wrapped her in a great big bear hug.

"Nice to meet you." Holly fought for air. Jeremy was six four if he was an inch, and built like something akin to the Hulk.

"Jeremy, you're smothering her." Sarah laughed.

"Sorry." Jeremy released her and stepped back. "Do you have any idea what a fascinating psychological study you two would make?"

"Jeremy . . ." Sarah warned. "This is my sister, not one of your guinea pigs."

"Sorry." Jeremy turned to Ben. "Are you the boyfriend?"

"The jury's still out on that one, I'm afraid. For now, I'm just a friend."

"Ben's a private investigator. I would never have found Sarah without him," Holly explained. "If at all possible, we hope to find our mother, or at least an explanation of what happened to her."

"Do you think you can?" Sarah asked. "Do you have any leads?"

"Just these necklaces." Holly handed them to Sarah. "They were in the two identical diaper bags that were found in the car I told you about."

Sarah studied the necklaces. Sapphires surrounded by diamonds in a custom setting. "They're beautiful."

"I thought maybe our mother knew she was having twins and bought them for us," Holly said.

"I doubt it. They look old. Older than us."

"Do you know anything about jewelry?"

"I know a little about art and collectibles. See this mark on the back? I'm pretty sure it's a jeweler's mark. It's like a signature. Maybe if you can find out which jeweler made them, you can find your next clue. Most jewelers who deal in custom pieces of this quality keep extensive records."

Holly took one of the necklaces and studied the back. "I never noticed that before."

"I know just the guy who might be able to help us," Ben announced. He set one of the necklaces on a table and took a picture of it with his cell phone. "I'll forward it to him after dinner. Are you joining us?" he asked Jeremy.

"I'd love to. Ladies?" He took each of the sisters by the arm.

Dinner was fun and lighthearted. Jeremy, like Ben, had a great sense of humor and kept everyone in stitches during most of the meal. The retelling of some of the experiments he had attempted that had gone horribly wrong left everyone weak with laughter.

"Don't believe everything he says. He's really a very good psychologist," Sarah clarified.

"When are you getting married?" Holly asked.

"In June, after we graduate. It'll be a small ceremony, just family and close friends. I want you to come."

"I'd love to."

"And you, too, Ben."

"I have an early day tomorrow," Jeremy announced. "I really should get home."

"Me, too." Sarah sighed. "This has been so wonderful. I can't tell you how happy all of this makes me. What do we do now?"

"I'd like to follow up on the mark on the necklaces and see where, if anywhere, that leads," Holly said.

"I have classes all week and then I go home," Sarah explained. "Let's exchange phone numbers. We'll keep in contact. Every day. If I have a mother out there, I want to find her, too. Either way, I want to stay in touch with my brand-new sister."

Ben and Jeremy walked to the parking lot ahead of the sisters, giving them time for private good-byes.

"Are you sure you have to leave already?" Sarah asked. "I have a pretty busy week, but I could make some time for us to hang out."

"As good as that sounds, I'm really anxious to finish this journey and see where it leads. If our mother is out there and I can find her, I have to try. Aunt Meg secured Ben's services through Christmas. Time is running out."

"Do you really think Ben is still helping you because of a bet?"

"No, I guess not. I'm sure he'll continue to help me as long as it takes, but I'm getting to the point where I need to finish this so I can get on with my life."

"And after you finish, then what? With you and Ben, I mean."

"I wish I knew the answer to that question. He says he loves me, but he's looking for happily ever after. I'm not sure I'm ready for that. But I can't imagine life without him either. I don't know what I want."

Sarah tucked a lock of hair behind Holly's ear. "You'll know; when the time is right, you'll know." She hugged her sister with all her might. "God, I'm going to miss you. I mean it—call me every day."

"I will."

"Promise!"

Holly thought of Noel and her similar unkept promise to her. "I promise."

"And if you find our mother, call me right away. I'll come, at any time. If she's still alive, I want to meet her together."

"I will."

Sarah hugged Holly one last time before wrapping her arm through hers and starting down the path to the parking lot.

Chapter 17

Thursday, December 12

Holly called Phillip the next morning. She'd found her sister, and she supposed she could catch the next flight to New York, but she knew in her heart that, in spite of the fact that syndicating her column was the second-most important thing in her life, finishing her journey with Ben was the most important.

As predicted, Phillip painted a doomsday scenario in which she'd not only lose the syndication deal but possibly her job. Holly knew that the scenario as portrayed should be enough to send her to the nearest airport, but it didn't send her running toward her past. She ended up telling Phillip in no uncertain terms that she was taking a leave until after the first of the year, and if her job and the syndication opportunity were still available, they'd talk about them then.

She had a few minutes before she needed to meet Ben so she called Noel and filled her in on everything that had happened since they'd last talked.

"You've had quite a couple of days," Noel said. "And Sarah sounds fantastic. I have to admit I'm a little jealous. Not that I'm not happy for you, but up until now I've been your sister."

"And you still are," Holly assured her. "My sister, my best friend, my everything. I want to have a friendship with Sarah, but I doubt we'll ever have what you and I do. We have a history. We're family."

"Thanks. That means a lot. And I want to meet your newest sister. I wonder who was born first."

"I doubt we'll ever know."

"Probably not."

"I'd better go. I'm pretty sure I just heard the shower in Ben's room go off. He'll probably be by soon."

"Still have two rooms, do you?"

"Yes," Holly emphasized, "we still have separate rooms. Ben and I are just friends. Well, maybe more than friends," she admitted. "I think I'm in love with him."

"And you don't want that?" Noel asked.

"I don't know. Maybe. I'm just not a hundred percent certain this is the right timing."

"Love isn't something you can analyze and figure out," Noel counseled. "I know you, and you'll put your relationship with Ben under a microscope to try to analyze ever detail. Love isn't always logical. It isn't always easy. It just *is*. Sometimes you have to make compromises and adjust your plans. But it's worth it. The details will work themselves out. Go with your heart. It won't let you down."

"Thanks, Noel."

Holly hung up, closed her eyes, and leaned back against the headboard of the bed. She let her mind wander to Ben: his breathtaking smile, his sexy body, his giving heart. She'd only known him a short time, but it felt like a lifetime. She couldn't imagine a life that didn't include him. Ben hadn't let her respond when he'd told her that he loved her, but Holly knew what she'd wanted to say. She loved him, too. It could never work, their lives were so different, but the truth of the matter was that the heart wants what the heart wants. Somehow, some way, they'd figure it out.

"Wake up, sleepyhead." Ben pounded on the connecting door, interrupting her thoughts. "I have breakfast."

Holly opened the door, allowing him to walk in and set a tray with fluffy scrambled eggs, golden toast, and hot coffee on the table beside her bed. "I would have let you sleep in a bit longer, but I got some news about the necklaces."

"You did?"

"The mark is from a jeweler in Dallas. I checked, and they place a unique mark on all of their custom pieces. I've made arrangements to meet with the owner of the jewelry store this afternoon."

"Do you think anyone will remember the necklaces? Sarah thinks they're pretty old."

"According to the gentleman I spoke to on the phone, they keep detailed records of all their custom work. Now, eat your eggs and we'll hit the road."

"This piece is quite old, before my time." The jeweler, a man in his midthirties with a receding hairline and sagging jowls, informed them five hours later. "My grandfather first opened the store eighty-five years ago. We've done quite a lot of custom work over the years. Both my grandfather and my father were sticklers for keeping detailed records, though, so I should be able to come up with some information for you. Check back with me in the morning."

"Thanks, we will." Ben jotted down his cell phone number on a piece of scratch paper. "Call me if you find anything before then."

As they left the store, Ben asked, "What would you like to do?"

"Christmas shopping," Holly suggested.

"Sounds good," Ben grabbed her hand and began walking down the street. "Where do you want to start?"

"How about that phone store?" Holly suggested. "I want to get a new cell for Jessica, and then I need to find something for Noel and her family. By the way, she doesn't hate you."

"She doesn't?"

"No. Tommy told her what happened a long time ago. She said she didn't try to fix us up because I hated every guy she set me up with. She figured we'd find each other on our own when the time was right."

"Smart girl."

"It seems that Aunt Meg's motives for sending you to help me weren't strictly about my finding my past. According to Noel, the two of them have been planning our eventual nuptials for a while."

Ben laughed. "I think I've been duped."

"Are you complaining?"

"Not a bit." Ben stopped walking and pulled her into his arms. "Remind me to thank Noel the next time I see her."

"The Winter Ball," Holly said as Ben lowered his head for an amazing yet quick kiss. "I promised her we'd come. I hope you don't mind."

"Actually, it sounds perfect." Ben looked into her eyes as he tucked a stray lock of blonde hair behind her ear. "My cabin can be very romantic in the wintertime. We'll pour some wine and watch it snow."

Holly felt her heart pounding as Ben lowered his head for another tender kiss that sent volts of longing through her body. She fought the impulse to suggest they skip the remainder of their quest and head for the cabin right now. She was about to do just that when Ben stepped back, kissed her on the tip of her nose, and continued down the street as if nothing earth-shattering had happened.

"When exactly is the ball?" he asked as he pulled her close to his side.

"The twenty-first." Holly tried to steady her breath. "It's strange to be looking at holiday lights and not have any snow. I wonder how much snow they have at home. Probably tons."

"In New York?"

"No, Moosehead, silly."

"Do you still think of Moosehead as home?" Ben asked.

"Yeah, I guess I do."

"Can you ever see yourself living there again?"

"Maybe. Are you asking me to live there with you?"

"Maybe."

"That whole snuggling-and-watching-it-snow thing is really tempting. On one hand, I want nothing more than to spend my life watching it snow with you. On the other, I have a job I worked really hard to get. If I moved to Moosehead, I'm not sure what I'd do. How about you? Your family is in New York. Have you ever thought about moving back?"

"Honestly, not once until now." Ben stopped walking. "With you, it would be more like starting a new life rather than living on the fringe of my old one. So maybe . . ."

Holly kissed Ben under the Christmas lights, with holiday music in the background and hordes of people moving around them.

"Are you hungry?"

"Starving."

"There's a really great pizza place near here," Ben suggested.

Chapter 18

Friday, December 13

Both Ben and Holly were awake early the next morning, anxious to find out whether the jeweler had any information that might help them in their search. When they arrived at the store, the jeweler was busy helping another customer, so they busied themselves looking around at the beautiful jewelry artfully displayed in locked cases.

"Some of this stuff must cost more than I make in a year." Holly stopped to appreciate the settings that complemented each jewel to its fullest. "They're really gorgeous, but honestly, I can't see myself wearing something so elaborate. This necklace looks like it must weigh twenty pounds, and that ring . . . I'd be afraid someone would cut off my finger to steal it. Personally, I prefer something simpler."

"Like what?" Ben asked.

"Well . . ." Holly wandered to another case. "Now, this is nice." She pointed to a diamond solitaire of moderate size. "A simple stone in a simple setting. I wouldn't want something I was paranoid about losing or damaging. Lord knows I have enough stress in my life."

"May I help you?" the jeweler interrupted.

"We were in yesterday inquiring about the sapphire necklaces," Ben reminded him.

"Oh, yes." The man walked out from behind the counter. "I have an address for you, but I'm not sure it's still valid. The woman who purchased the necklaces did so over forty years ago." He handed

Ben a piece of paper with a name and address written on it.

"The note in the file said the woman bought the necklaces for her twin daughters," the man added. "If you look at the signature on the back of the necklaces, you can see that they're slightly different. This one has a *C* woven into the mark, and the other has a *V*."

Holly tried to make out the slight variation the man was referring to. The letters weren't evident until the man handed her a magnifying glass. The craftsmanship was intricate and detailed, indicative of an accomplished artist.

"I see what you mean. Do we know what the letters stand for?" Holly asked.

"Constance and Vivian. Those are the names of the two daughters."

"Thank you so much for your help." Ben shook the man's hand. "Do you have a business card in case we have any other questions?"

"Certainly."

"What now?" Holly asked as she walked out of the store and into the warm sunshine with Ben at her side.

"I'll call a buddy of mine and see if he can track down the current whereabouts of the woman who originally bought the necklaces. We might as well check out the address while we're waiting, but to be honest, after forty years, it's a long shot."

They hailed a cab and traveled uptown to the apartment building indicated on the slip of paper. It was a bright and sunny Friday, warm for December. Residents were out and about, enjoying the beautiful morning: jogging, walking dogs, pushing baby carriages, and talking to neighbors across the neatly trimmed hedges that separated one building from another.

"Wait here." Ben instructed the cab driver as he jogged to the building's intercom.

"I'm looking for Prudence Stillwell," Ben said when he pushed the button for apartment 2B.

"No one here by that name," a male voice answered back.

"Sorry for the inconvenience."

Ben returned to the cab. "No luck."

"Where to now, mister?" the cab driver asked.

"Shopping," Ben answered. "We never did get much done yesterday. This may be our last chance. If my contact comes through, we'll probably be back on the road by tomorrow."

"I really wasn't looking forward to the holidays this year," Holly admitted as they walked around the festively decorated store. "But this is fun. So who's on your list?"

"My mom and Marty are really hard to buy for—they never seem to need anything—so I thought I'd get them tickets to that new musical that's opening after the first of the year. Then there's my eldest sister and her husband, as well as their daughters, Amber, Jade, and Ruby."

"Wow. Your sister must really like jewels." Holly stopped to sort through a table with discounted cashmere sweaters.

"Actually," Ben handed her a blue one he particularly liked, "she was reading a book while she was pregnant with Amber in which all the daughters in a family had jewel names. She liked the idea, so she borrowed it."

"It's a good thing she had girls. Who else is on your list?" Holly held up the sweater in front of her, then decided the neckline was too low to wear to work.

"There's my sister Lisa, and her husband Alex, as well as their daughters, Hallie, Hannah, and Hayden."

"Again with the theme names." Holly found a turtleneck in a soft shade of fawn and held it up to her chest as she glanced into a nearby mirror. "You wouldn't by chance have any preconceived ideas of what the names of your own offspring might be?"

"I'm going to name them after famous New York Yankees."

"What if they're girls?" Holly set down the sweater and looked directly at Ben.

"It can work. Lots of girls have guy's names."

"I see." Holly put her arm around Ben and headed toward the escalator in the center of the store. "Anyone else on your list?"

"Just my youngest sister, Carolyn. She's still single."

"How about your sister who died. Peg. Did she have a family before . . ."

"No. The force was Peg's family. Talk about a workaholic. She was dating one of the guys she worked with, though, so who knows? If she hadn't died, they might have gotten together."

"Any ideas of what you might get everyone?" Holly asked as they stepped onto the moving stairs.

"I thought I'd get each of my sisters a gift certificate for a day at a spa. The full-pamper treatment. And I'll get their husbands tickets to a Yankees game next spring. That just leaves my nieces, and I have no idea what to get for them. I used to get dolls across the board, but some of them are getting a little too old for those."

"How old are they?"

"Amber's twelve, Hallie's eleven, Jade is ten, Hannah is eight, Ruby is six, and Hayden is five."

"Toys are probably the most appropriate for the younger three, but maybe clothes or a video game for the older ones would be better," Holly suggested. "And there's always makeup. Kid makeup," Holly clarified. "Glittery lip gloss and nail polish. They'd all probably like that. The children's department is on this floor. Let's have a look and see what we can find. "

After searching through the many aisles of the store, they settled on sweaters for all six girls, cute theme ones for the younger ones and more sophisticated ones for the older girls. They also bought glitter makeup for all six, as well as cute purses to put it in.

"I'm done in record time," Ben said as they stood in line at the cash register of the accessories department. "I'm going to have these packages wrapped and mailed to my mom's house. Once I do that, I'll help you with your shopping. Do you want to come with me to gift wrap, or do you want to look around and meet up in an hour or so?"

"I think I'll get started. How about we meet in the restaurant in an hour?" Holly suggested.

"Sounds good." Ben kissed her firmly on the lips before heading into the crowd in search of the gift-wrap department.

Holly decided to take the opportunity to look for something for Ben. But what did one get for someone she had only known for a little over two weeks but might quite possibly spend the rest of her life with? A shirt or sweater seemed too impersonal. She really had no idea what his interests and hobbies were. He liked the Yankees. Maybe a cap? No, that didn't seem right either. Boxer shorts? Slippers? Cologne? Maybe a watch?

Holly spent the entire hour she had before meeting Ben looking through floors of festively displayed goods to meet the needs of every taste and budget, but still was clueless as to what would bring a smile to Ben's face on Christmas morning. Maybe she'd call Noel. She had a husband she had to shop for every year. Or maybe Ben's mom? Holly could just picture how that conversation might go: "Hi. You don't know me, but I need a romantic gift idea for your son."

No, Holly decided, Ben was her friend, and she'd figure out something to get for him on her own. Friend? That seemed like an odd word to use to describe the relationship she had with Ben, but for the life of her, she couldn't come up with a better one. They weren't even dating, so something more definitive like *boyfriend* or *significant other* didn't seem quite right. *Soul mate* seemed too retro, although if Holly were honest with herself, it felt the most accurate of the aforementioned options.

"Can I help you?" an older gentleman with a full head of white hair and a kind smile asked.

Holly realized that she had been standing in the middle of the store staring blankly at a rack of ties. "Uh, no thanks. I was just trying to figure out what to get for my—" Holly hesitated. "For Ben."

"A friend?" the man asked.

"Yes, a *good* friend," Holly emphasized.

"You appear to be bagless," Ben commented as he kissed Holly and held out a chair for her an hour later.

"I got distracted."

"I see. Can I help?"

"Noel needs a new blender," Holly improvised. "She told me so the last time I spoke to her. I thought I'd get her one of those fancy ones with all the speeds and attachments. I also thought I'd get several bottles of alcohol and mixes. Noel likes her blended drinks. I actually thought I'd give that to Noel and Tommy as a couples gift. For the kids, I thought we could go to the toy store down the street after we eat. I want to pick something up for Bobby, and his sisters, too."

"Sounds like a plan."

Ben's phone vibrated on the table between them. He glanced at the number on the caller ID. "It's Kurt, my contact. I should get this."

Ben excused himself and left the restaurant. Several minutes later, he returned with a smile on his face. "We have a phone number and address for Prudence Stillwell."

"Do you think it's the same one?"

"Probably. This Prudence lived in Dallas during the time the necklaces were made. She also gave birth to twin daughters forty-eight years ago."

"What now? Do we call her? Or should we go to see her?"

"She's living in Malibu, California, now," Ben informed her. "I suppose we could call her."

"What if we call her and she has something to hide? I don't want to scare her off before we have a chance to see what, if anything, she knows. I say we go to see her."

"I agree. A personal visit may be the best course of action at this point. If we leave now, we can be there by the day after tomorrow."

"You're going to need a new car after this."

"I'll definitely need an oil change," Ben agreed.

Chapter 19

Sunday, December 15

Ben pulled up in front of a cream-colored, two-story house nestled on a hillside overlooking the Pacific Ocean. Roses, dormant on the vine, lined the walkway between the driveway and the covered front porch. The expansive lawn surrounding the house was neatly trimmed and the extensive gardens meticulously groomed.

Holly got out of the car and stopped to take a deep breath as she looked out over the ocean in the distance. It was such a beautiful day. The sun shone bright in the sky, glistening on the water as surfers paddled out in search of the perfect wave. With temperatures hovering around the mid-seventies, it didn't seem like December at all.

Although the house didn't sit directly on the beach, it was close enough to the water for the occupants to enjoy the sound of crashing waves and the smell of salt in the air.

"Are you ready?" Ben asked as he helped Holly out of the Range Rover.

"I guess I'm as ready as I'll ever be." Holly clung to Ben's hand as they walked up the brick walkway.

He rang the doorbell. Holly could feel her heart pounding as the seconds ticked away. A dog barked. A voice commanded it to be quiet. The lock from the dead bolt turned. The door slowly opened, and an attractive elderly woman dressed in a long gray dress stood staring at them.

"Oh my," the woman whispered, before falling to the floor in a dead faint.

Ben pushed the door open and Holly crouched down at the woman's side.

"Are you okay?" Holly cradled her head in her lap, gently touching her wrinkled cheek as the woman opened her eyes.

"Constance?" The woman was barely breathing.

"No, I'm Holly. Did you hurt yourself? Can you get up?"

"Here, let me help you," Ben offered. He lifted the woman from the floor and helped her over to a sofa.

The woman sat, white as a sheet, staring at Holly without speaking.

"Can I get you anything?" Holly asked. "Water? A cold rag?"

"Who are you?" the woman demanded in a slightly stronger voice.

"Holly Thompson. And this is Ben Holiday."

"Why are you here? What do you want? Is this a trick of some kind? I'm an old lady with a weak heart, and this isn't at all funny."

"No. No trick, I promise. We just wanted to ask you about these necklaces. The jeweler who made them said that you bought them for your daughters." Holly took the jewelry out of her pocket and handed them to the woman.

"Where did you get these?"

Holly looked at Ben. "I was found in a car that had been in a major accident when I was an infant. The other occupants of the vehicle died in the resulting fire, but a passerby pulled me out, along with two identical diaper bags. These necklaces were inside the bags."

The woman gripped the necklaces with all her might. "Oh my God." Tears streamed down her weathered face as she stared at Holly.

Holly sat down next to her and placed her hands over those of the sobbing woman. "Are you okay? Is there anything I can do?"

The woman sobbed louder.

"Find some tissues," Holly instructed Ben.

He walked down the hall in search of the requested item while Holly tried to comfort the woman. Maybe they should have called first. Holly hoped the shock of their visit hadn't been too much for the poor woman. She hated to be responsible for the obvious stress she was causing.

The woman cupped Holly's face and looked directly into her eyes. "My baby. I never thought I'd see you."

"Do you know who I am?" Holly whispered.

"Yes, I think I do."

Ben returned with Kleenex.

The woman briefly closed her eyes and offered a prayer of thanks before opening them and taking the offered box. "Give me a minute to pull myself together and I'll tell you what I know." The woman stood up. "There's a fresh pitcher of lemonade in the refrigerator. The kitchen is down the hall and to your left. Holly, be a dear and fetch us each a glass while I freshen up." She straightened her back, smoothed her hair, and regally walked down the opposite hallway.

"Wow, way to recover." Holly stood up and walked with Ben toward the kitchen.

"The woman obviously has upper-class breeding. I doubt she's used to falling to pieces in front of total strangers. In fact," Ben speculated, "I doubt she's used to falling to pieces at all. She seems like a European aristocrat."

"I see what you mean. Look at this place. It's neat to the point of perfection. And she's dressed like someone who's getting ready to go to afternoon tea at the royal gardens. You don't think she was on her way out, do you?"

The kitchen was large and modern, and so spotlessly clean that it looked like it had never been used. They began looking through neatly arranged cabinets for glasses for the lemonade.

"I don't know. I guess if she really had to go, she'd say so. These should do." Ben pulled three tall crystal goblets out of an overhead cabinet.

Holly retrieved the promised pitcher of freshly squeezed juice from the refrigerator and then hesitated. "Do you think she meant us to bring the drinks into the living room, or are we supposed to move to the dining room or the breakfast nook?"

"I noticed a small sunroom directly off the entry when we came in. It has a view of the ocean. Let's try that," Ben suggested. "It looked cheery and inviting, and it had a table and sofa."

"Just set the drinks on the table there," Prudence directed them when she found them in the sunroom, carrying a large book in her hands. "I usually take my tea here."

Holly poured the lemonade and set the three glasses on the table. Prudence settled in the middle of the sofa and Ben and Holly sat down on either side of her. She pushed her glass forward and opened the book, a large photo album, in front of her.

"I believe this is your mother."

The picture Prudence was pointing to was of a young woman who looked exactly like Holly.

Holly gasped but didn't say anything. She'd imagined that finally finding her mother would be an emotional moment, but nothing could have prepared her for the myriad of emotions that gripped her as she looked at the face of the woman who had given her life for the first time.

"Her name was Constance. Connie," the woman corrected. "She preferred Connie."

"Was?" Holly ran her index finger lovingly over the face that could have been her own.

"She disappeared a long time ago. I never knew what happened to her. She was pregnant when she left. I guess you must be that baby."

"Babies," Holly said. "I have a sister, a twin sister: Sarah."

"Twins." Prudence seemed to be lost in memories of her own. "Connie was a twin. Her sister's name was Vivian. Oh, how happy I was when they were born. My life felt so complete. They were beautiful, perfect. I bought the necklaces for them when they were only a few months old."

"And Vivian?" Holly asked.

"She was killed in an automobile accident when the girls were sixteen. It was late, an icy winter evening. Vivian was riding home from a dance at the club with some of her friends when the car went off the road. Everyone was killed."

Prudence wiped a tear from her cheek. "Constance should have been in the car with them that night. If she weren't so strong willed, she would have been. You see, while Vivian was a lot like me— proper, cultured—Constance was a free spirit, a rebel.

She hated the dances at the club and, on this particular occasion, refused to go. We fought about it, but in the end, I tired of the battle and gave up. Instead of going to the dance, she went off with some of her friends to a poetry reading in a coffee shop uptown."

"I'm sorry." Holly placed her hand over Prudence's arm. "It must have been difficult to lose a child."

"I was devastated. So was Constance. If anything, our grief tore us farther apart. After Vivian died, Constance was convinced that I secretly wished it were she who had died instead of her sister. It wasn't true, of course, but Connie believed it to be, and it drove a wedge between us. The truth of the matter was, Connie had an energy, a spirit, I often found myself envying, longing for," she continued. "I had been brought up the same way I was bringing up my own girls: proper, repressed. Like Vivian, I spent my youth attending piano recitals, afternoon teas, and boring charity events."

Prudence turned the page of the photo album. "I didn't have Connie's daring. Although I longed to shed the trappings of my upbringing, I didn't have the courage to do so. Eventually, I even managed to convince myself that the trappings of my station in life were exactly what I wanted."

The page to which Prudence had turned showed a smiling girl in various stages of her youth: flinging herself into a body of water from a rope swing; running through a meadow with a litter of puppies, covered head to foot with mud and grime; twirling under a sunny sky with her arms outstretched and her hair flying wildly.

"Looks like someone I know," Ben commented from the opposite end of the sofa.

Prudence stared at the page as a single tear slowly coursed down her cheek and onto the page. "I loved Vivian. I enjoyed spending time with her. But I respected and admired Connie. No one could tell her what to do or how to live her life."

She pulled herself together and sat up taller. "Shortly after Vivian's death, Constance came to me and told me that she wanted to go to school in San Francisco. She still had another year of high school but managed to pass a proficiency exam that would let her start college early. My heart was empty after Vivian's death and I no longer had the strength to battle with Constance, so I let her go. She came home to visit a few times after, but our relationship became that of alienated strangers. I can't tell you how much I've regretted that every day of my life."

"What happened? How did she . . ." Holly hesitated, "What events led to our birth?"

Prudence took a sip of her lemonade and straightened her already perfectly groomed bun. "Three months into what I believed was Connie's final year of college, she turned up on my doorstep, very pregnant. I was stunned beyond belief, to say the least. Women in our family simply didn't have children out of wedlock. She told me that she needed to stay with me until after the baby was born. From where I was sitting, it looked as if that was going to be any minute, so I invited her in and she settled into her old room. I tried to get her to tell me who the father was, but she absolutely refused to talk about him. In fact, she pretty much refused to talk at all. She mostly stayed in her room and stared at the ceiling. She seemed distraught, fearful."

Holly watched the changes that came over the woman's face as she fought for control of her emotions. She must have been beautiful in her day. She still was, but years of grief and guilt had taken their toll.

"I had no idea what was going on in her mind, or what had happened to turn my vibrant child into a fearful recluse, but I was desperate to do something, anything, to fix things and get back to normal, whatever normal was. My next move, my solution to my perception of the problem, was one that I have regretted every day since. I'm afraid it sealed both our fates.

"I contacted a friend of mine, an attorney who worked for a private adoption agency," Prudence continued. "I arranged for a representative of the agency to meet with Connie to discuss her options. It seemed that a quiet adoption would fix everything. Connie could go back to school and finish her education, and no one in our circle of friends would need to know about the whole sordid affair. Of course, Connie didn't see things that way. I should have known she wouldn't. She was gone the next morning, and I never saw her again." Another tear worked its way down the weathered cheek of the woman who had lived all these years with so much pain.

"She left a note saying that she needed time to work things out, and that I shouldn't try to contact her," Prudence said. "I honored her request for a while, and then I started to put out a few feelers. They never turned up anything."

Holly sat quietly, trying to gather her own thoughts. "I'm so sorry. I can't imagine how horrible it must have been for you." She touched the woman's hand, and looked deeply into eyes as blue as her own. "I've fantasized about my mother, but not once did it occur to me that I might have a grandmother. I hope we can be friends."

The older woman began to sob, and Holly hugged her tightly. The pair rocked gently back and forth as they mourned the loss of the woman they had lost and the miracle that had brought them together.

Ben discreetly excused himself while grandmother and granddaughter forged a bond of blood and shared ancestry. When he returned to the sunroom, the pair were looking through the photo album, laughing as if they had known each other forever.

"What about my father?" Holly asked. "You said my mother never told you who he was, but might she have left any clues? A diary? Letters?"

"I don't know. After awhile I had all of her things boxed up. Everything is in the attic. I've never gone through any of it, but you're welcome to look."

"That would be great."

Prudence led Holly to the attic, which was equally as neat as the rest of the house. "Connie's things are in the far corner."

There were several stacks of boxes with a *C* written on the side. Next to them were similar stacks marked with a *V*. Holly took several boxes from the top of the pile and set them on the floor. She began opening lids and sorting through books and personal mementos.

"I'm afraid it's a bit chilly up here for my old bones. I'll wait for you in the sunroom." Prudence turned and walked back down the stairs.

Ben and Holly spent the next twenty minutes sorting through the boxes. Holly was sorry she didn't have more time to really look through the photos and mementos left by her mother. It was sad to think that a lifetime of memories could be reduced to a few boxes.

"I think I found something." Holly held up a thick journal stuffed with loose pieces of paper, ticket stubs, and other mementos. She opened it to the back. "The last journal entry is dated December fifteenth." She began to read aloud.

> *Mother wants me to give up my babies, but I'll never do that. How does one simply give away something so precious? My babies are as much a part of me as my heart and soul. I can't believe how much I love them already. I feel kicking and moving about, and I know that my heart will never be mine alone again. I think I finally understand how devastated Mom must have felt when Vivian died. To lose a sister, especially one who is literally the other half of oneself, is painful beyond belief. But to lose a child . . . I haven't even met mine, but I know that their loss would be worse than death itself. I wish I could stay and try to make Mom understand how much these babies mean to me, but I think it's best that I go. I don't know what the future will bring, but once the danger has passed, I hope I am able to return and rebuild what is left of my*

family. Patrick would have wanted his babies to be part of a large, loving family.

"Patrick?" Holly asked. "Patrick who? And what danger?"

"Go back a few entries and see what else the journal says. See if you can find out where she first mentions being pregnant," Ben suggested.

Holly turned through the pages, skimming for the first mention of her pending motherhood. "Here's an entry dated in late July."

Dr. Evergreen confirmed what I already knew in my heart. Patrick and I are going to be parents. I am filled with both a joy beyond anything I have ever known and a bone-chilling fear of how Patrick will take the news. He thinks his family won't approve of our relationship. I guess I can see his point. A twenty- one-year-old bride probably wouldn't help his political aspirations much. But I know he loves me, and I hope that will be enough.

"Do you think his family broke them up?" Holly asked.

"I don't know; keep reading."

Holly flipped to another page, dated a few days after the pregnancy had been confirmed.

I have a secret that has filled my heart with such joy that I feel it will burst, yet I can't tell anyone. Today Patrick made me his wife. It was a small ceremony, just the two of us and the minister. I wish Mom could have been there. We haven't always gotten along, but I love her and I know she would have wanted to be there for this sacred event. Patrick doesn't want to make our union public until he has a chance to talk to his family. He is leaving to go overseas in a few days, so we have decided to keep our secret until he returns. I know that his parents are hoping he will be our next senator, and having a wife fifteen years his junior is bound to be a detriment, but our love is ageless, and I hope once they get to know me, they'll see that's true.

Holly flipped through a few more pages. "Oh God. Listen to this entry from early November."

My despair is so great that I feel like I can't breathe. I'm not sure how I will go on. My instinct is to simply close my eyes and fade into oblivion. Patrick's plane went down over China today. I'm told there were no survivors. I can't imagine continuing to live in the world without him. As much as I want to swallow the entire bottle of sedatives the doctor gave me, thus ending my torment, I know that I must be strong for our babies. I can't do this alone. I think it's time I went home.

"There's a newspaper article." Holly handed it to Ben.

"'Patrick Harrison, eldest son of Reginald Harrison, founder of Harrison Industries, died today when the private airplane on which he was a passenger crashed over a remote part of China. A spokesperson for the company reported that Mr. Harrison had been in China as the last stop in a twelve-week tour of the company's international facilities.'" Ben stopped reading and stared at Holly. "Your father was Patrick Harrison? Of Harrison Industries and Harrison Aeronautics? He must have been worth millions when he died."

Holly paled. "Millions?"

"If Patrick loved your mom enough to marry her, chances are he planned to make her a beneficiary to his estate, which could explain the danger she referred to," Ben pointed out. "It would make sense that if he did write a new will, whoever the beneficiary of the old one was could have reason to feel threatened by your mother's existence. Although we don't know whom, if anyone, Patrick may have told about his marriage prior to his death. I doubt it was well known, since the newspaper article doesn't mention a wife."

"You think someone killed my dad to protect his inheritance?" Holly asked.

"It must have been a lot of money," Ben pointed out.

"Okay, then who ended up inheriting Patrick's money?"

"Good question." Ben pulled out his phone and walked over to a window, where his reception was better, while Holly continued reading the journal.

It seemed so odd to read the personal thoughts and feelings of the woman who had given Holly life. She wished she could have met her. It sounded like they were a lot alike. Prudence had said that Connie was a free spirit who knew her own mind, and evidence in the journal indicated that she had been determined to march to the beat of her own drum. There were stubs from concerts tucked into the pages of the journal, along with programs from poetry readings held at a coffee house near the college she attended, and references to philosophers she had read and enjoyed. In the center of the journal, a few pages behind the entry about their wedding, was a copy of her marriage license, as well as a copy of a new will naming her the heir to his personal estate.

"Patrick's brother Paul was the sole beneficiary to Patrick's stock in Harrison Industries, but someone named Courtney Anderson inherited his personal assets: money, houses, cars, that sort of thing," Ben informed her after he hung up his phone. "The will that was presented at the time of his death was over eight years old. If Patrick made a new will after his marriage to your mother, it was never brought forward."

"He wrote a new will." Holly handed him the documents. "It's dated a week before Patrick left for his overseas trip, naming my mother and his unborn child as co-heirs to his personal estate."

Ben looked over the will, then turned to Holly. "Paul seems to have inherited the stock in Harrison Industries in both the old and new will, so it's only Courtney who was disinherited."

"Do you think she had anything to do with Patrick's death?" Holly wondered.

"I don't know. It seems far-fetched, but something strange went on. Your mom finds out she's pregnant and marries her millionaire boyfriend. They decided to wait to announce the news until after he returns from a trip, but he never makes it back. Meanwhile, your mom delivers you and Sarah but is so afraid for your lives that she sends you away with total strangers. The whole thing is too bizarre to be mere coincidence."

"Let's assume that somehow Courtney found out about the new will. Who else would know?" Holly asked.

"The lawyer," Ben answered. "Maybe he and Courtney had a thing going on. It would help to know exactly who this Courtney is and what her relationship to Patrick was."

"Can we find that out?" Holly asked.

"We can." Ben took out his phone once again.

"Do all of your contacts ever wonder why you want all the information you do?" Holly wondered.

"I don't know. I've helped most of them out more than once. I never ask when they need help, and they never ask when I do."

"Wow, you have really good friends. That says a lot. If you were a creep, or maybe some closet serial killer, you wouldn't have so many people willing to jeopardize their jobs and reputations to help you out."

"Still don't trust me?"

Holly smiled. "A girl can never be too careful."

Ben made his calls and found out that Courtney Anderson had been Patrick's ex-fiancée. He had abruptly broken things off with her when he met and fell in love with Constance. And after Patrick died in China, Courtney inherited Patrick's personal assets and married his attorney, Evan Rolland.

"So the heir to the estate in the old will and the attorney who wrote the new will married. Sounds like motive for murder to me," Holly asserted.

"We need to find out why your mom was in Gardiner. Maybe your grandmother has some idea. We should ask her."

"Did you find what you were looking for?" Prudence asked when Ben and Holly emerged from the attic.

"Partially," Holly answered. "I was wondering if you knew why Connie would have gone to Gardiner, Montana, when she left here?"

"Her father's brother, Carl, lived there," Prudence answered.

Later that evening, Ben and Holly walked barefoot down the beach. Prudence retired early after they returned from a dinner out, so they had the evening to themselves. "It's so peaceful and relaxing." Holly wrapped her arm around Ben's waist as they walked along the water's edge.

"I guess we should head back," Ben said. "It's gotten chilly since the sun went down."

"Yeah, and I want to call Sarah before it gets too late."

"I noticed that Prudence had a small deck off the attic overlooking the water. I bet the view from up there is fantastic. How about we pick up a bottle of wine on the way back to the house, bundle up, and sit outside for a while?" Ben suggested. "It's been a while since I've been to the coast. I'd forgotten how relaxing the sound of the waves can be."

"Sounds perfect."

When they returned to the house, Ben went into the kitchen to pour the wine, while Holly put on a sweater, then went out onto the deck to talk to her sister. "Ben left a message for Paul earlier. He thinks our uncle might be able to fill in some of the blanks."

"Like what happened to our mother?" Sarah asked.

"Exactly."

"Is there anything that proves our story?" Sarah wondered. "He may think we're just after the money if you contact him with the announcement that he has two long-lost nieces. I'm sure when you're as rich as the Harrisons, you get a lot of whack jobs looking for a way to cash in."

"I have a copy of our parents' marriage license," Holly informed her. "There were also photos of our mother with a man who I assume is Patrick in the box of stuff at our grandmother's house, and of course we have the copy of the new will," Holly added.

"I guess that should be enough. Are you thinking of going to see him?"

"I guess." Holly sighed.

"You don't sound very excited about the prospect of a new uncle."

"It's not that. I guess I'm just tired. I feel like I've been trapped in a movie-of-the-week for a while now. When I started this journey, I felt somewhat in control of my own destiny, but somewhere along the way events that were totally out of my control seem to have taken over. Part of me wants to get this all figured out. Part of me wants to wrap everything up nice and neat, answer all the questions, cross all the *t*s, dot all the *i*s. But another part of me wants to go home to Moosehead, go to Noel's silly dance, and then crawl into bed, pull the covers over my head, and not come out until after Christmas."

"I know what you mean," Sarah agreed. "Jeremy wants us to get away and just relax for a couple of days, now that the semester is winding down, but I know I should go home and see my mom. I've talked to her on the phone at least twenty times since she was here, but she still seems frantic. I've assured her time and time again that I'm going to be okay with things, but I don't think she believes me."

"Why don't you come to Moosehead for New Year's?" Holly asked. "Bring your mom, and of course Jeremy. I'll invite Prudence, I mean Grandma. I wonder if she wants to be called that? Anyway, I have this huge house that Aunt Meg left me, and you can all stay there. I'll even have someone go in and air it out. We'll have a big party, and I'll introduce you to my foster sister, Noel, and her family. It'll be fun."

"I would like to meet our grandmother," Sarah admitted. "And the New Year sounds like it's going to be a little more exciting than I had originally planned, so some good old-fashioned fun might be nice. I'll have to talk to my mom."

"Is that Sarah?" Ben asked when he came up to the deck.

"Yeah. Why?"

"Put her on speaker."

"Ben wants me to put you on speaker," Holly informed her sister.

"Hey, Ben," she said as soon as Holly switched the phone.

"Hey, Sarah. I just got a call back from your Uncle Paul. He wants to meet you both, and he doesn't want to wait until after the New Year. He wanted to have a chance to check on a few things and tell his parents about your existence, but he was wondering if you could meet somewhere convenient for the two of you within the next week or so? I didn't commit one way or the other. I told him I'd ask and call him back, but he seemed overwhelmed with joy when I told him who you were."

"Really?" Holly was happy but surprised. "Mom's journal made it sound like our father's family wouldn't be happy about his relationship with her."

"I guess when a brother and son dies, you tend to look at things a bit differently. So how about it? Should I tell him you're willing to meet?"

"What do you think?" Holly asked Sarah.

"Wow, an uncle and grandparents, possibly an aunt and cousins. I'd love to meet them. I really should go home and see my mom for a day or two but then, yeah, I'm game."

"Should I set something up for the weekend?" Ben asked.

"The ball is on Saturday," Holly reminded him. "I promised Noel. Christmas is on Wednesday, and I usually spend Christmas Eve and Christmas Day with her also."

"Yeah, I should be with my mom for Christmas also. But any other day is fine with me," Sarah added.

"Okay, I'll call him back and set something up."

Chapter 20

Monday, December 16

Holly awoke the next morning to the sound of waves crashing in the distance. It must be nice to live at the ocean. She enjoyed her life in New York, but sometimes she missed waking to the sound of something other than traffic. Slipping her feet into her slippers, she pulled on a robe and headed downstairs.

"Good morning." Prudence was already up and dressed in a shin-length housedress and sturdy heels. "I hope you slept well."

"I did. Thank you." Holly sat down at the table next to her new grandmother.

"Would you like some coffee?" Prudence offered.

"I would. I can get it. You don't need to get up."

"Nonsense, dear. I haven't had anyone to wait on for quite some time. I find that I miss the experience." Prudence set a cup of hot coffee in front of her. "Would you like cream and sugar?"

"Black is fine."

"I have some fresh berries I got from the farmers market. I thought maybe you'd like some with your breakfast."

"You have a farmers market in December?"

"In sunny California we do. I picked up some fresh eggs as well, if you'd like an omelet."

"I think I'll just start with coffee. It usually takes my digestive system a while to wake up. Where's Ben?"

"He said he needed to make some calls, so I told him he could use the phone in my study. The cell service at the house tends to be sketchy at times."

"It really is beautiful here. Have you lived here long?"

"Almost thirty-five years," Prudence answered.

"So my mom lived in this house?"

"She did. In fact, the room you slept in last night used to be her room. I kept all of her things for years, hoping she'd come home, but when she never did, I got rid of everything, including the furniture, and created a guest room. It was easier to start fresh than it was to try to remodel what I'd always thought of as hers. At one point, I thought about selling the house and starting over altogether, but I guess a small part of me still hopes that she'll show up on my doorstep one day."

"I can understand that." Holly took a sip of her coffee. "Still, this is a big house for one person."

"It is," Prudence agreed. "I like my home, and the view is exceptional, but at times it gets lonely. My closet neighbor, who was also my best friend, passed on last year. It's been hard living up here on the hill without her to drop in on me from time to time. I've been thinking about selling, but with the way the market's been, I figured it'd be best to wait."

"Do you travel much?" Holly wondered.

"Not really. I guess I'm a bit of a homebody. I have a few friends in town and I volunteer for several organizations, so I keep busy."

"Sarah is coming to Moosehead for New Year's," Holly informed her. "I'd love it if you could come as well. I have a big house with plenty of room."

Prudence smiled. "I'd like that very much."

"We'll make the arrangements before we leave. I'll plan to pick you up at the airport."

"It's been a while since I've traveled north. I guess I'll have to buy some warm boots. Your mother's dad used to tease me about my impractical footwear when we lived in Denver for a short while. I was brought up to dress a certain way, which did not include heavy boots and feather jackets."

"Is he still alive?" Holly wondered. "My mom's father."

"He is. His name is George, and he lives in Portland. We divorced when the girls were young, but we've remained friends. I'm sure he's going to be thrilled to find out that he has granddaughters. I should call him."

"Invite him for New Year's as well," Holly suggested. "Unless it would be strange for you to have him there."

"No, it wouldn't be strange. As I said, we've remained friends."

"Morning." Ben walked into the room. He kissed Holly on the cheek before refreshing his own cup of coffee. "I have news," he announced.

"News?" Holly asked.

Ben sat down at the table across from Holly. "Last night, while I was speaking to Paul, I mentioned that Rosa had said that someone by the name of Smitty was the person who was chasing your mother. Paul said he knew who Smitty was and intended to track him down. I just spoke with Paul, and it seems he was successful. It took a bit of doing, but Paul was able to convince Smitty to tell him everything he knew."

"Does he know what happened to my mother?" Holly asked.

"Not exactly. It turns out that we were correct in our assumption that it was Courtney who wanted you and your mother dead. Before your father left for his trip overseas, he notified Courtney of his marriage to your mother and the change to his will. According to Smitty, he asked her to keep it to herself because he wasn't ready to tell his family, though he thought it only right that he inform her right away, since the change affected her in a significant way. Smitty said that Patrick and Courtney had been together for ten years and engaged for two, so she took the news really hard. She couldn't understand why Patrick would leave her for someone so young and was certain that the affair would burn itself out and Patrick would return to her."

"I hate to admit it, since she tried to have me killed, but I sort of feel sorry for her," Holly said.

"I sort of do, too. I guess after Patrick died, Courtney went a little bit insane. Smitty said that her grief turned to rage, and she somehow convinced herself that your mother was responsible for everything that was wrong in her life. She let her rage drive her over the edge, and she hired Smitty to 'take care of things.'"

"She ordered him to kill us," Holly emphasized. "What sort of person would take a job like that?"

"A hired gun," Ben explained. "Smitty worked security for Harrison Enterprises before ending up in prison. He'd only been out a few weeks when Courtney hired him, and he claims he was desperate for money, which clouded his judgment. He figured he could take care of the whole thing in a few hours and use the money he earned to start over somewhere new."

"But my mom was one step ahead of him," Holly guessed.

"Smitty told Paul that when he went to the apartment your mom had been living in, she was gone. He found a message on her answering machine from a friend of Courtney's, warning her that Courtney was on a rampage and that it might serve her well to make herself scarce. Smitty looked through her desk in an attempt to find out where she'd gone and found a letter with your address on it." Ben nodded to Prudence.

"That must be when she came home," Prudence realized.

"According to Smitty, he managed to track her movement from her apartment to your house and then to her uncle's in Gardiner. His orders were to kill both Constance and her baby, but by the time he caught up with her in Gardiner, she was gone. Carl Langley was dead on the floor and the bed was covered in blood, but your mother was nowhere to be found. He figured that given the amount of blood on the bed, there was no way she could have lived."

"And after that?" Holly asked.

"He stripped the bed and went home. He used the sheets as proof that things were taken care of. Courtney married Evan Rolland, the attorney who drew up the new will, and Smitty was paid handsomely for his part in the affair. He moved to the Bahamas, which is where Paul tracked him down. I guess he made him an offer he couldn't refuse, so he agreed to fly back to San Francisco and talk to the police."

"I can't believe it's been twenty-seven years and no one ever suspected anything," Holly stated.

"No one other than Courtney, the attorney, and Smitty even knew of your mother's existence, so no one questioned it when Evan produced the old will, naming Courtney as beneficiary. Paul knew she had been Patrick's fiancé, and although he knew they were having problems in their relationship, he didn't know about your mother and so had no reason to think Patrick might have changed his will."

"What about the friend?" Prudence asked. "The one who warned Connie?"

"He was killed in a single-car accident the day after he left the message. Smitty told Paul he didn't know for certain whether Courtney was responsible for the accident, but he wouldn't be surprised. Paul notified the police, who have picked up Courtney for questioning. Paul is pretty certain she'll be charged with a variety of things, including hiring Smitty to commit murder."

"And Evan Rolland?" Holly wondered.

"He drowned in a boating accident four months after he married Constance. The incident was declared an accident, but the authorities may reopen the case in light of recent developments."

"So my mom could still be alive? If Smitty didn't kill her, she could have gotten away."

"Perhaps," Ben agreed. "I've put out some feelers. It would help if we had a photo of Connie." He looked at Prudence.

"Of course. Do you really think it's possible? Could my Connie still be alive?"

Ben took her hand in his. "It's actually pretty unlikely. It seems if she was alive, she would have contacted you at some point, and we know she never went looking for her babies, so I think we should assume she's dead."

Prudence looked down at the table.

"Having said that, I intend to continue to look until we have confirmation one way or the other. I suppose it's possible she did live but didn't contact you or go looking for her babies because she feared for your safety. I guess the only way we'll know is to find out what happened to her after she left Carl Langley's."

"Thank you." Prudence wiped a tear from her eye.

"In the meantime," he turned to Holly, "I've arranged for you and Sarah to meet with your Uncle Paul later this week. He's going to meet us in Saint Paul."

"Does Sarah know?"

"I called her to confirm the date and time. She's flying home today, and Paul has booked a flight to Saint Paul."

"I guess we should head back ourselves." Holly turned to Prudence. "We still have a couple of days of driving ahead of us. I'll call you right away if I hear anything about my mother."

"I'd appreciate that."

"And I'll see you for New Year's." Holly felt like she was going to cry. She'd just found her grandmother and she hated to leave her, but she really needed to get home if she was going to keep her promise to Noel to attend the ball.

"Absolutely."

Chapter 21

Friday, December 20

"I can't believe how nervous I am." Holly held Sarah's hand as they waited in the lobby of an elegant hotel in Saint Paul, Minnesota.

"Does it seem odd to you that they asked Ben and Jeremy to go in ahead and asked us to wait here?" Sarah wondered.

"Yeah a bit," Holly agreed. "I think something is up. Ben has been on the phone a lot, and he told me that he had some business to take care of and was gone for most of the day yesterday. By the way, I love your dress."

Sarah smiled. "Yeah, I like yours, too. I can't believe we both chose to wear red. I mean it is Christmassy and all, but still . . ."

"We share the same blood." Holly squeezed Sarah's hand more strongly. "I guess it's not all that odd that we share similar tastes."

"I wish they'd hurry up and do whatever it is they're doing," Sarah complained. "The longer we sit here, the more nervous I get."

"As nervous as I am at this minute, I'm not half as nervous as I was the day I went to the university to find you," Holly confessed. "I was afraid you'd hate me."

"Hate you? Why?"

"Oh, I don't know, for totally messing up your life and shattering everything you knew to be true about who you were and where you came from."

"I could never hate you." Sarah hugged her. "This is going to sound strange, but even though I never knew you existed, I think I've always missed you. It's like I knew something was missing."

"I know exactly what you mean. When I watched the tape Meg left me, I was so angry that she'd kept this huge secret from me, but deep down inside I realize that on some level I'd always known there was someone in the world who belonged to me."

"You never said *why* she never told you about me," Sarah commented.

"She said she was scared. That she was waiting for the right time, but somehow that time never came."

"Yeah, that's basically what my mom said as well."

"Are you doing okay? The two of you?"

"Yeah. I was really upset at first, but I guess I understand why she did what she did. I do wish she hadn't messed with my birthday on the birth certificate she forged, though. It's going to take me a while to get that straightened out."

"Ben thought it was because she wanted you to be able to start school a year earlier."

"Yeah, that's basically what she said."

"Here comes Ben." Holly stood up.

"Ladies." Ben held out both arms, one for each sister to hold as he escorted them into the restaurant.

"What were you talking about all this time?" Holly asked.

"You'll see." Ben grinned.

"Oh God, he has a secret," Holly warned Sarah. "I'd recognize that grin anywhere."

"Not sure I can take any more surprises," Sarah teased.

"By the way, happy birthday to both of you." Ben placed a hand on each sister's back as he showed them through a door into the reception area of a large office.

"I celebrate my birthday on December 24," Holly reminded him. "The day they brought me to Meg."

"Yeah, and I celebrate mine in May, although I guess I should think about changing that."

"Yes, but today is the actual day of your birth," Ben informed them.

"How do you know that?" Holly wondered.

"You'll see." Ben grinned as he opened the door to the office where not only Paul waited, but a woman Holly supposed was his wife, seven young adults of varying ages, whom Holly figured must be cousins or possibly cousins-in-law, an older couple she hoped were Patrick's parents, Sarah's mom Rosa, Prudence, who stood next to a man in his late sixties or early seventies, and a woman probably in her late forties, who looked to be the spitting image of Holly and Sarah. Next to her stood a man, also in his forties, and two young girls in their teens. There were tears on the faces of every one of the room's occupants, as both Holly and Sarah stood speechlessly studying the group.

"I'm your Uncle Paul." The handsome man in the center stepped forward and hugged both girls. "I can't tell you how happy I was when Ben called and told me that my brother had left behind two beautiful daughters I never knew existed."

"We're—" Sarah started.

"Overwhelmed," Holly finished.

"I want to introduce you to everyone, but first I have a birthday gift for you," Paul continued.

Prudence stepped forward with the middle-aged woman by her side.

"Mom?" Holly gasped.

The woman tried to speak but instead burst into tears as she hugged both her daughters.

"We thought you were dead," Sarah sobbed.

As Holly and Sarah hugged their mother and wept, the others gathered around. Prudence and her ex-husband, Connie's father, George; Paul's wife and children; Rosa; Paul's parents, Reginald and Phyllis Harrison; and their mom's second husband, Gus, and her two teenage daughters, Hilary and Gracie.

After everyone had been introduced, Paul led the group toward a private banquet room, where they could enjoy a meal while continuing to get to know each other.

"What happened after we became separated?" Holly asked her mother when she was seated with Sarah at a small table in the corner of the room. "Why didn't you ever look for us?"

"It's kind of a long story."

"We have time," Holly encouraged.

"Your delivery was a difficult one. I lost a lot of blood and almost died. I didn't remember it at the time, but after you were born, I tried to divert Smitty's attention away from the vehicle in which you left by driving in the opposite direction. I must have passed out. I woke up in a hospital several weeks later. A passing motorist took me there, and although I was all but dead, they managed to save my life. The problem was that I couldn't remember anything. I couldn't remember my name, or how I came to be left half dead on the side of the road. The doctor knew I had recently given birth, but I couldn't remember anything about the birth or a child I might have delivered. The doctor said that amnesia isn't uncommon when someone goes through the physical and psychological trauma I had obviously undergone. While I was recuperating, the police checked local hospitals, but I hadn't been admitted to any of them. I didn't have any type of identification on me, so the authorities were having a heck of a time figuring out who I was and where I had come from. I'd never been arrested or had a government job or any other reason to be fingerprinted, so even though they searched for a while, they never could identify me."

"But you remembered?" Sarah asked. "Eventually?"

"No, not until Paul and my mother showed up at my door a few days ago. I guess Ben found an old police report detailing the investigation when I was first found. After a thorough search, everyone gave up, and the paperwork was filed away with other unsolved cases. Once Ben realized that there had to be a record of me either dead or alive somewhere, he called in a bunch of favors and patched the pieces of the mystery together. Since I didn't remember anything, even after being told what had happened, Paul arranged to have my mother brought to me. The moment I saw her standing on my porch, everything came flooding back."

"It must have been so awful for you to wake up and not know who you were," Holly sympathized.

"It was. I was terrified. I didn't know anyone and had no idea what I was going to do. My husband Gus was one of the police officers assigned to my case. We developed a friendship while I was in the hospital, and after I was released he took me home with him because I had nowhere to go. Over time we fell in love and had the girls."

Holly looked across the room to where her two younger half sisters and their father were visiting with Prudence and George.

"As time went by, I built a new life and rarely thought about the old one. I knew I'd had a baby, so I worried that there was a husband somewhere looking for me, but as weeks turned to months and months turned to years, I managed to let go of the horror I felt those first few months and enjoy the life I had."

"And now that you remember, does it change how you feel about the life you've created?" Sarah asked.

"No, not really. Your father died a long time ago. I will always love him, but I have Gus, and he's wonderful. Realizing that I have four children instead of two is a blessing, and while I guess on some level I mourn all the lost years, I realize that no matter how much I'd like things to be different, I can't have those years back. This whole thing must be completely overwhelming to the both of you," Connie said, squeezing both their hands.

"A bit," Holly confessed. "It's just hard to get my head around everything, if you know what I mean."

"I absolutely know what you mean. When Paul and Mom showed up at my door and my memory came rushing back, I was so frightened. I mourned the loss of the life I'd once known and didn't know what this new information was going to do to my new life. And I had to explain everything to the girls, which really terrified me. Gus and I had never told them about my memory loss or the fact that I must have a history that I couldn't remember. I was afraid that news would be overwhelming to them, and in truth, it was a little dicey at first. They were hurt that I hadn't told them sooner."

"But everything is okay now?" Holly wondered.

"Yes, after I explained they understood. Besides, after Paul filled them in on the financial side of my past life, the girls were thrilled. They've been dream shopping cars ever since. Of course, neither of them is old enough to drive, but that's not stopping them."

"So the money you were supposed to inherit—it's still there?" Holly asked.

"Paul is sorting it all out, but yes, all three of Patrick Harrison's heirs are going to do quite nicely. Any idea what you both might do with your share?"

"I have a huge list of research projects I've wanted to pursue if I ever had the money." Sarah smiled. "I can't wait to get started—" she glanced toward Jeremy, who was talking to the cousins— "after my honeymoon, that is. How about you, Holly?"

"Me?" Holly looked around the room and realized that she already had her secret wish and desire, a large family that actually belonged to her. She looked at Ben, who was laughing at something Grandpa Harrison had said, and realized that there wasn't a single thing in the world that she wanted or needed that she didn't already have. And then she thought of Bobby, and felt a tug on her heartstrings. "I think I'll build a family."

Chapter 22

Monday, December 23

"Happy?" Ben asked as he guided the horse-drawn carriage through the freshly fallen snow. They'd made the trek through the festively decorated town and were returning to Ben's lakefront home through the narrow forest trail.

"Very." Holly leaned her head on Ben's shoulder as she snuggled under the blanket he'd thought to bring. "Although," Holly added, "as romantic as this is, I find myself wishing Bobby and the girls were here. Poor kids have been through enough pain and suffering this past year. It'd be fun to give them a good old-fashioned Christmas."

"I talked to Bobby's grandmother yesterday," Ben volunteered. "It seems like things are going pretty well, but she's going to have to have an operation in a couple of weeks and won't be able to keep them after that. I know it's only two days till Christmas, and it'll be nearly impossible to find airline tickets, but I was thinking that maybe we could fly them out now, let them spend the holidays with us, then find them a permanent home after the first of the year."

"I love the idea." Holly smiled. "And I've been thinking about a permanent placement." Holly turned so that she was looking directly at Ben. "I think I'm going to apply to be their foster parent."

"You? Really? Are you sure?"

Holly brushed the snow off her shoulders. "I'm sure. I have that big house Meg left me. The house was built to provide a home for kids in need. I figured

I might as well fill it up. It's what Meg would have wanted."

"But what about your job? New York?"

"Apparently, I've just come into some money, so I don't think that quitting my job will be all that big of an issue," Holly teased.

"That's not what I meant."

"I know. My job means a lot to me. I worked really hard to get to where I am, and I think I really help people. I talked to my boss, Phillip, who admitted that the syndication deal he'd been working on isn't dead, and I talked to Jessica, who has done a stellar job of covering for me while I've been away, and she's agreed to become a full partner. If I can get Phillip to agree, I figure I can write the column from here, and with Jessica in the New York office, things will be covered. I may have to fly to New York once a month or so, but I think it can work."

"Are you sure about this?"

"Aunt Meg changed lives. What she did was important. I don't know where I would have ended up if it hadn't been for her. Bobby and his sisters are good kids with a lot of potential. If they end up in the wrong place, a place that won't nurture Bobby's intelligence and independent spirit, who knows what will happen to them?"

"It's a big responsibility. Raising three kids will be hard and messy and loud. You'll have no privacy and very little time to yourself."

"Which is exactly why I plan to hire help. Aunt Meg did it all herself. I'm not sure I can do that. I plan to use part of my inheritance to hire a housekeeper, and maybe a couple of nannies to keep an eye on things."

"Sounds like you've been thinking about this a lot."

"I have. I really want to do this, and as it turns out, I have an immediate opening for a personal assistant. You wouldn't happen to be interested in the job?"

"Personal assistant. How personal?" Ben began to nuzzle her neck.

"Oh, very personal."

"I don't know. I'm going to have to think about it. It's a big decision," Ben teased. Holly's smile faded. "I'm kidding." He kissed her. "Of course I want the job. As long as it comes with a lifetime contract."

"I think that can be arranged."

Epilogue

"Anyone seen Ben?" Holly asked the group of women gathered in the kitchen of the old farmhouse. It had been two years since she'd begun her life-altering journey, and in that time, so much had changed.

"He was building a snow fort with some of the boys the last time I saw him," Sarah answered.

Holly looked out of the window, but all she saw were Bobby, and his foster brothers and new friends.

"He might have gone upstairs," Rosa offered. "I overheard Becky asking him if he'd come to her tea party. I can look if you want."

"Thanks, I'd appreciate that. Stephanie should be up from her nap, if you can grab her while you're up there," Holly said. Eighteen-month-old Stephanie Garwood had only been with them a few weeks and was the newest member of their growing family. Bobby, his dog Dusty, and his sisters Becky and Annie, had been with them for two years, and Timmy Randall and Frankie Longwood had joined them the previous winter.

"I love your decorations," her mom commented. It had been strange for Holly to start thinking of her mom as Kate, when she had already grown used to thinking of her as Connie, but as she had pointed out, she'd been Kate for more than half of her life and everyone, including her husband and daughters, was used to that name.

"Thanks. Most of them were Meg's, but I've added a few of my own. Each of the kids picks an ornament to add to the tree each year they're with us.

It's nice to have something to remember those who move on to other placements by."

"How are Theresa and Celeste doing?" Kate wondered.

"Really well." Holly smiled. The sisters had only been with them for eight months, but in that time, she'd grown to love them. "They're back with their mom, who has completed rehab and is working for the Baptist Church as a housekeeper. Theresa started middle school this year, and I've been told that she's thriving in the advanced placement classes they offer."

"I'm glad everything worked out for them. They're both such nice girls. They still send me a letter every now and then."

"How many place settings do we need?" Noel asked as she started gathering plates to set the table.

Holly did a quick calculation in her head. While her own twin sons, Reggie Jackson Holiday and Joe DiMaggio Holiday, were barely three months old and too young to need a place setting, her six foster children, Noel's four children, and her two half-sisters, Hilary and Gracie, added up to twelve bodies at the children's table. Once you added in Ben and herself, Noel and Tommy, Sarah and Jeremy, Rosa, Kate, Gus, and Prudence, that brought the total to twenty-two.

"Twenty-two, I guess." Holly opened the oven to check on the turkey.

"Maybe it's a good thing Ben's family decided to come when the babies were born and your Uncle Paul and his family decided to wait until after New Year's," Noel pointed out. "If everyone had come at once, you would have had to set up tables in the barn."

"I have to admit it's a little crowded, but somehow it seems sort of perfect." Holly smiled. "I enjoyed spending last Christmas with Ben's family in New York, but Moosehead is home. I find that I really like having everyone here for the holidays."

"Do you think this will be enough gravy?" Sarah asked.

"Add a little more water to thin it out," Kate advised as she tossed the green salad.

"You needed me?" Ben wandered into the kitchen from upstairs.

"Dinner is almost ready. Can you round up the boys?"

"Anything for my beautiful wife." Ben kissed her lightly on the lips before pulling on his down jacket and heading out of the back door.

"Such a charmer," Kate commented. "He reminds me of your father."

"My father was a charmer?" As happy as she was to have found her mom and a large extended family, it made her sad that she'd never have the chance to know her father. Her Uncle Paul had shown her photos and told her stories of their childhood together. They'd had all the advantages of being from a wealthy family who traveled the world and engaged in exotic adventures.

"He was." Her mom's eyes twinkled. "I remember our first Christmas like it was yesterday. We'd only just met and weren't yet a couple. I was still in college, and he'd come into town for a conference. We met at a coffee shop downtown while we were both shopping for Christmas presents. The restaurant was full, so he invited me to share his table. We spent an hour comparing the gifts we'd bought and the gifts we'd yet to purchase. I remember how my heart pounded as he laughed at my tales of shopping mishaps and gift disasters. Somewhere between my soup and his sandwich, I fell in love with the most charming man I had ever met."

Holly smiled. "That's so sweet. Love at first sight. It must run in the family."

"Or not." Sarah laughed. "Jeremy asked me to go out with him for a solid year before I finally agreed. I can assure you there was no love at first sight at play in our relationship."

"Why a whole year?" Holly asked.

"I thought he was a dork."

"Dork?" Holly laughed. "But he's so sweet."

"Yeah, in a nerdy sort of way." Sarah giggled. "Don't get me wrong; I love Jeremy. But when I first met him, I thought he was too much of a screwup for a serious student like me. I was planning to become a world-renowned physicist and he was still going to keg parties and lighting farts. You didn't know him then, but let's just say he's matured over the years."

Holly laughed. "Lighting farts?"

"Who's lighting farts?" Ben brushed the snow from his shoulders as he came in through the kitchen door. Holly's heart skipped a beat as his shaggy hair draped over one eye. "If it's Timmy, I already warned him about that."

"No one is lighting farts," Holly assured him. "Did you round up the boys?"

"Bobby, Brian, Cody, and Timmy were building a snow fort. They're on their way in, but Cassidy and Frankie are nowhere to be found."

"Check the barn," Holly suggested as she slid the rolls into the oven. "Frankie has been asking about a sleigh ride all day. I told him that we were going to wait until after dinner, but you know Frankie . . ."

In the nine months Frankie had been with them, he'd been a challenge. He was on his fifth foster home in three years, and somewhere along the way he'd learned that waiting for good things to happen never really worked out. If he wanted a cookie, he took a cookie. If he wanted to swim in the pond, he swam in the pond. Chances were if he wanted a sleigh ride, he was hitching up Buck and Betty as they spoke.

Can I help?" Jeremy asked as he opened the refrigerator in search of a beer.

Holly had to fight a giggle as she pictured Jeremy performing his act of arson. "There are a stack of folding chairs in the basement near the door, if you could bring them up," Holly instructed.

"I'll help," Gus offered, popping the cap off his own pale ale before following Jeremy down the stairs.

Holly began gathering the red glassware Meg had used every year for Christmas Eve dinner for as long as she could remember. Meg's everyday dishes were usually plastic or paper in deference to the number of kids at the table at any one time, but every Christmas Eve she'd break out the dinnerware that she'd told Holly her mother had bought during a trip to Europe.

"Girls are coming," Rosa said, coming into the kitchen. "Prudence was doing their hair. I've been informed that I am to remind you that Annie doesn't want mashed potatoes. She says they make her puke."

"Already on it," Holly assured her. "Annie doesn't like potatoes, Becky won't eat green beans,

Timmy is allergic to tomatoes, and Annie won't eat meat. Check, check, check, and check," Holly recited.

"It looks like you have this mothering thing down pat." Kate hugged her daughter.

"I wouldn't say down pat, but I'm learning. It's been a tough couple of years, with the new syndication deal followed by eight kids and a remodel. But once the holidays are over, Ben and I plan to spend a glorious week out at the lake house before heading to New York for a week."

"You're taking the babies?" Kate asked as she scooped mashed potatoes into a large ceramic bowl.

"Yeah, they're too little to stay with Molly and the girls," Holly said, referring to her housemother, Molly Stevens, and the two assistants who ran things on a daily basis. After they were married, Ben and Holly had decided to adopt Bobby, Becky, and Annie, who had been living with Holly since that first Christmas. When they decided to take on additional foster children looking for temporary placement, they were prepared for minor conflicts and a period of adjustment. But when Holly found out she was pregnant with twins, she was afraid the addition of biological children to the blended family would cause feelings of resentment and insecurity. It turned out that she'd worried for nothing. All the kids loved their new baby brothers, and the jealousy she was afraid would rear its ugly head had never materialized.

Ben and Holly loved all of the kids and they knew it. The kids adored Molly and weren't at all upset that she attended to their daily care. Molly and her assistants had been given two weeks off over the holidays so they could spend time with family, but after the first of the year, Holly would gladly return to spending her days working on her column while Molly attended to the house and the kids.

"Do you remember how you used to call me crazy for having four kids?" Noel reminded her. "You have twice that many. Who's crazy now?"

Holly laughed as something crashed. The noise, which sounded a lot like breaking glass, seemed to be coming from the dining room, where Noel had just finished setting the table.

"Do I want to ask?" Holly looked at Ben, who jogged into the kitchen in search of a broom and dust pan. By this point, all three of the family dogs were barking at whatever catastrophe had occurred.

"Timmy and Toby had a little accident," Ben explained. Toby was the resident golden retriever.

"Accident?"

"Timmy was trying out his new sled, and Toby was chasing him down the hill. Frankie opened the door just as he got to the bottom and Timmy thought it would be fun to see how far he could glide into the living room rather than stopping when he got to the porch."

"He ran into the table," Holly guessed.

"It's not too bad. Toby got a head full of stuffing and Timmy is going to have a bruise on his lip, but they're fine."

"And the rest of the dishes?"

"Survived the crash," Ben assured her.

"Should I dish up another bowl of stuffing?" Noel asked.

"Yeah. There's plenty in the big pan in the warming oven. Let's get this show on the road before something else happens, though. Everything is ready and I don't want it to get cold."

"Are you planning to attend services tonight?" Prudence asked as she wandered down the stairs with Becky and Annie on her heels.

"Yeah, although we'll need to speed things up a bit. I promised the kids they could open one present each before we headed to town in the sleigh. I still need to change, and Ben has to hook up the horses."

"Do you have room for all twelve kids?" Prudence wondered.

"We have room for all of us if everyone wants to go," Holly assured her. "Meg always had a houseful over the holidays, so she made certain she had the biggest sleigh the horses could manage. She never wanted to let anyone down by not having enough of something, which is a trait I guess I took from her."

"Which explains all this food." Prudence laughed. "We have enough to feed an army."

"Don't be so sure," Holly commented. "Kids eat a lot, and we have a lot of kids."

"You're taking the boys in the sleigh?" Prudence asked.

Holly knew she was referring to Joe and Reggie, and not the other six boys in residence.

"I can bundle them up. If you want to hold one and Mom wants to hold the other, I'll settle you on the backseat, where the other kids won't climb all over you."

"I'd love to help." Prudence smiled.

Ben and Holly sat on the front porch, wrapped up in one of the patchwork quilts Meg had made before she died. Every year Meg would gather together all the clothes her crew of children had worn out and make a quilt. Some of the quilts she kept, others were given to her kids when they left for permanent homes, while most were donated to the homeless shelter in town.

The kids, all eight of them, were fast asleep with visions of Santa Claus and dancing sugar plums in their dreams. Callie, the resident huge orange cat, was curled up on Holly's lap, while resident canines Dusty, Toby, and Willa snored gently as the pair rocked back and forth on the old swing. The full moon was shining down on the freshly fallen snow that had blanketed the area for most of the day.

Holly pulled the quilt tightly around them as their breath hung on the cold air. It was a toasty thirty-one degrees, a virtual heat wave for a winter's night in Minnesota. Holly knew the forecast called for a drop in temperature over the next few weeks, so when Ben suggested a glass of wine before they dug into the chores they had left after their visitors departed, she suggested they sit in the swing while they had the chance.

Bright white lights were wrapped around every door and window, making the old farmhouse look like something you'd find in a fairy village. Christmas carols played quietly on the stereo just inside the front door, creating a backdrop for the otherwise silent night. Holly smiled at the snowman family the kids had built that afternoon. There were ten figures in all, one for each member of the family.

"I still have two bikes and three wagons to put together." Ben yawned.

"Hmm," Holly answered tiredly.

"Luckily, Gus assembled the dollhouse Annie asked for while the kids and I were playing in the snow. I don't know what these toy manufacturers are thinking. The blueprints for the dang thing were so complicated, I never would have patched the contraption together if Gus hadn't offered to help."

"I suggested we pay the extra twenty dollars to have it assembled at the toy store," Holly reminded him.

Ben smiled. "Next time remind me to listen to my smart wife. By the way, did you ever manage to find that doll Becky wanted?" Ben caressed Holly's hair as she leaned her head against his shoulder.

"If I confess to calling in a favor and getting it directly from the manufacturer, will you think any less of me?"

Ben laughed. "No. It's actually kind of nice to have a wife with toy-store connections."

"After spending three weeks trying to find the doll, and then eventually calling a guy I met while I was doing a story a couple of years ago, I realized the pressure advertising puts on parents at Christmas. I found myself wishing there really was a Santa."

"Maybe there is." Ben kissed her neck.

"Two bikes and three wagons," she reminded him.

"It's early," he said, nuzzling her shoulder.

"It's after eleven. I can guarantee the kids will be up by six."

Ben groaned but pulled away.

"My grandmother seemed to really enjoy the church services tonight," Holly commented. "She told me that she used to sing in her church choir, but after Vivian died she lost her faith and stopped attending church altogether. She mentioned that the church in Malibu is large and sort of trendy. I don't know this for certain, but I wouldn't be surprised if she was living in Moosehead by this time next year."

"You think she wants to move here?"

Holly shrugged. "She didn't actually say it, but she hit it off with Reverend Collins, and I heard him mention what a beautiful voice she had. Grandma actually blushed, and I overheard her say that if she were going to join a church, it would be a little hometown church like he had. He told her that a woman as fine as herself would be an asset to the community."

"You think she's going to move halfway across the country to go to church?"

"No, silly. I think she's going to move halfway across the country because she found out she has a granddaughter and two beautiful great-grandsons who would love to have her close by. I think she's going to move halfway across the country because of the spark I'm certain she felt when she met Reverend Collins. And I think she's going to move halfway across the country because she's alone in Malibu and now that she's found her family, she never wants to be alone again."

"If you want her to move here and she wants to move here, then let's get her moved," Ben said. "After the first of the year. It'll be nice to have her close by. If there's one thing you've reminded me of, it's that family should be with family."

"I was sorry Bobby's grandma couldn't make the trip," Holly said. "We'll have to take the kids for a visit as soon as things settle down a bit."

"She won't even know them," Ben teased. In the two years Bobby and his sisters had been with them, there had been huge changes in their behavior and personalities. The girls were more outgoing and Bobby was more subdued. Becky, who was afraid to talk to anyone she didn't know when she first came to live with them, not only joined the Girl Scouts but the local softball team as well. Annie, who used to do nothing but read quietly in her room, was now a member of the Moosehead Children's Theater, and Bobby, who had made the biggest change of all, was not only well behaved but usually took it upon himself, as the oldest child, to make sure that the other members of the household were well behaved as well.

"I know what you mean. Remember when we first picked Bobby up? He was so bitter, and he told me that he didn't believe in Christmas."

"I remember."

Holly ran her nails over Ben's jeans-clad thigh as they slowly rocked back and forth. "We were decorating the little trees the kids wanted for their rooms, and he asked me what I wanted Santa to bring for me. I told him that I was too old to ask for anything from Santa. He gave me a hug, looked me in the eye, and said 'you're never too old for the magic of Christmas.'"

Kathi Daley lives with her husband, kids, grandkids, and Bernese Mountain dogs in beautiful Lake Tahoe. When she isn't writing, she likes to read (preferably at the beach or by the fire), cook (preferably something with chocolate or cheese), and garden (planting and planning, not weeding). She also enjoys spending time on the water when she's not hiking, biking, or snowshoeing the miles of desolate trails surrounding her home.

Visit Kathi:
Facebook at Kathi Daley Books
Twitter at Kathi Daley@kathidaley
Webpage www.kathidaley.com

FEB 0 1 2014 MN

Made in the USA
San Bernardino, CA
05 December 2013